WINE

DARK

DEEP

Book Two:
ENCOUNTER AT JUPITER

R. Peter Keith

Sleep, delicious and profound,
the very counterfeit of death.

Homer, The Odyssey

One

Cal woke with a start, sweat burning down his spine. The ship was quiet, the firing of its main engine having ceased days ago. His quarters at the very top of Red Hab had a strip of windows running across the ceiling. Outside those strips of transparent material, the orange and white sphere of Jupiter rose and set twice per minute: the spin rate of the *Ulysses*'s huge centrifuge arms.

He sat up in his bunk, mopping the sweat from his face with his blanket, and turned to place his feet on the cold plastic flooring. Jupiter cast orange light through the windows, throwing fast moving shadows across his floor. The shadows hid the silver briefcase he had carried with him during his recent escape from the asteroid miners.

He let out a deep breath, grabbed the jumpsuit he had worn the day before, and wriggled into it while staring up at Jupiter. He stepped out of the door of his quarters and into the cramped central corridor of the habitat: a closet-like room with doors on four sides and an open ceiling through which rose a metal ladder.

The ladder extended up through the habitat. He climbed through the four floors, gravity receding with each rung, toward the ship's spine. When the ladder reached the limit of the habitat structure, it ended and was replaced by a collapsible nylon rope ladder that stretched through the tunnel of the centrifuge arm. He pulled a motorized device from the wall

1

and clasped it to the rope to let it tow him up through the dwindling gravity to the zero-G hub. From there he guided himself through the storage area by pulling on handrails and sailing down the central corridor of the ship into the sparkling lights of the command module.

Through two great angling cockpit windows, framed by an array of lights and screens, the Jovian planet shone bright and still. No longer under thrust, the *Ulysses* continued along on the grand orbit it had escaped to while blasting its way out of Ceres's orbit. The Jovian world was still millions of miles away, but it's pull would eventually bend the ship's path so that, with the aid of a few course corrections, *Ulysses* would swing right around Jupiter. Bleeding off enough velocity, the interplanetary ship would loop back around the planet and into a stable orbit.

Ulysses was approaching the giant planet from its sunward side, gaining on the Jovian as it swept along on its 4300-day orbit. The ship sailed through an area of space encompassing a group of asteroids that numbered in the millions. They shared Jupiter's orbit around the sun; the so-called Trojan asteroids. Primeval remainders of the early solar system, they are dragged along within stable space sargassos: Jupiter's Lagrange points. The calms in the eye of the storm caused by a war between Jovian gravity, centripetal forces, and the gravity of the sun.

One set of space rocks preceded the king of planets, and the second set trailed behind. The interplanetary ship hurtled through the space around L5—the trailing Lagrange point.

There were millions of such rocks in the trailing swarm. Despite this, the sky in front of them was basically empty apart from the Jovian and its wispy rings. Such was the vastness of space. Only every once in a while would Cal spy a space rock or two librating away.

Although the danger of collision with larger objects was small, the odds of hitting something tiny were pretty great—there were billions more grains of dust and debris in any given cubic meter of this space than in the Main Belt around Ceres. The interplanetary ship had powered and extended its protective electromagnetic fields and was bathing the area ahead of them both with radar and wide-field infrared beams in order to spot potential problems, presumably in time to avoid them.

Two

On the periphery of the incredible volume of space that enclosed the Trojan swarm, an oblong piece of space debris about half a mile wide rotated lazily on its long axis. It had been classified as a binary asteroid, like its larger neighbor 617 Patroclus, because it was thought to be two objects orbiting a shared center of gravity. In this particular case, one of those two objects happened not to be an accretion of dust, rock, and ice. In fact, it was tethered to the other space rock by wisps and splays of material distributed in fractal swirls linking the two masses. These geometric armatures were in the process of breaking down. Whorls and gouts of the material were sloughing off from the asteroid and drifting away. This development had begun days earlier, triggered by the probing touch of radar and infrared beams.

Three

Xu Zuoren sat in the right-hand seat of *Ulysses*'s command module. His view was filled with the majesty of the yet-distant Jovian and its system of moons and rings. They fanned out around the world like glittering bands of jewelry, but Xu ignored it; he knew better views were to come. So engrossed was he with his screen that he was startled when someone slid into the left-hand seat.

"Still can't sleep, Cal?" Xu asked, eyeing his groggy-eyed commander.

"I sleep, I just don't stay asleep."

"Another nightmare?"

"Dream. A dream. One of those dreams where nothing happens, but it's still terrifying."

"A rose by any other name is still a nightmare."

"Okay, nightmare," Cal said. "In the dream, I'm just walking through a winter forest. Nothing scary about that. It has to be about . . . what happened down there. I never dreamt anything like this before Ceres."

"Why do you insist on confiding in me? The Doc would love it if you'd talk to her."

"Yeah, I know she would. I don't want to open that can of worms." Cal switched his attention to the windows that Zuoren had open on his console and changed the conversation. He pointed at the ship's projected course. "Anything close and or big enough to worry about?"

"Nothing Odysseus hasn't already adjusted for. We have time before we reach radiation zones intense enough to need to retract the habitats."

The Quindar tone reserved for AI communication sounded from the cockpit speakers and a window burst open on the face of Xu's console. "Telescope panorama three-five-twenty-three complete."

"Thank you, Odysseus." Zuoren paused, paging back and forth between screens. "Go ahead and commence the next sweep and focus the main telescope on the secondary radar search area please."

Four

The object broke free from its sheltering partner and tumbled away slowly. It trailed tendrils of fractal shapes, remnants of the connections that had joined it with the asteroid for an interminable span of time. With no visible sign of power other than its very movement, it slowed its tumble and began to accelerate toward the gas giant. As it shrank away from its longtime partner, the larger rock began to drift apart from itself, falling to pieces like an empty shell collapsing.

Five

Another set of windows, linked in a 3D arrangement, bloomed on Zuoren's console and commanded his attention.

"Captain. . ." he said, trailing off. He slid another window over the 3D arrangement and watched the transformations. ". . . earlier this morning, Odysseus reported something interesting. I adapted some relative photometry techniques and made a comparison between a particular asteroid and two other nearby Trojans in order to give us a good baseline for the examination of a phenomenon we are witnessing."

"And what, exactly, are we witnessing?"

"Most likely a collision between two objects. The first being 300242-DZ70, a binary asteroid made up of a three-and-a-half-mile long potato-shaped rock and its much smaller moon. We passed within one hundred and twenty-five miles of the pair three days ago. It was likely struck by another as yet unknown object, resulting in the disintegration of the larger of the binary's two masses over the last thirty-six hours and creating an expanding spherical debris field."

"Hmmm."

"Odysseus is comparing radar, infrared, and telescopic imaging sweeps to see if we can identify anything that might be responsible for the destruction of the binary, but so far we haven't located anything."

"And what about this debris field, could it pose any danger to the *Ulysses*?"

"Unlikely sir, unless by coincidence debris is caught up in Jupiter's gravity and ends up on an intersecting orbit with us some time in the future."

"All right then, what about this asteroid's moon?"

"That's where things get really interesting," Zuoren said, and swiped the window on his console into an image that appeared to float between the captain and himself. "There's something different about the remaining companion."

"How so?"

"As you recall, albedo is the measurement of the ability to reflect light," Zuoren said.

"Thanks," Cal whispered, genuinely grateful to Zuoren for the refresher.

"It tells us that the surface of the companion moon is different. The other rocks in the area have an albedo similar to that of a comet's nucleus—a dark, space-weathered surface with traces of organic compounds. Same for the remains of the shattered asteroid. The companion, however, has a high albedo."

The image changed.

"It's much brighter, likely consisting of different materials or of similar materials but formed much more recently."

"That is interesting."

"Indeed, as is the interesting coincidence that, out of all of the fragments of this collision expanding into space, the moon alone is headed directly toward us."

"That *is* interesting."

"It is. Analysis made of the last few days' worth of data indicate that it is moving, exactly toward us, at a greater speed than any model of asteroidal collision would predict."

"This word *interesting* is beginning to fail us."

"Yes, it is."

"Telescope?"

"Trained on the anomaly since Odysseus noticed the debris field."

"Put it up throughout the ship, please."

Cal reached over and tabbed the ship-wide communications

channel. "People . . . We have an unexpected and interesting phenomena occurring directly in our wake. There is an object, an apparent product of an asteroid breakup that—" Cal looked over at Xu for a moment before turning back to the panel. "That may or may not be headed toward us."

"Open ship-wide chat."

"Roger, Captain," Inez said.

"Putting it on the main comms feed," Zuoren said. Windows popped open on the screens in the command module, both habitats, and the docking and engineering rings. Along the top of the window a time lapse strip showed the breakup of the binary and the expansion of the debris field. Along the bottom of the window another time lapse—a magnification of the moon.

"It just looks like any small space rock," commented Inez.

"Yeah, nothing particularly interesting about it to me," the Doc said. "Not that it's my expertise or anything. Maybe some of the debris trailing it looks a little odd? Maybe."

"That's a pretty bright rock," said Samuels.

"Precisely," Xu said. "You will notice that before whatever caused the event that we are calling an asteroid collision, the binary and its moon seemed to have nearly identical albedo values."

"And after the collision or explosion, not so much."

"Correct, Captain. After that, it registers as a much brighter object, it is possible that a thick layer of dust was disturbed by the collision."

"Explosion."

"Probably not, Pilot. The outer layer seems to have been shed over a period of hours, see? It's here on this sweep, we see swaths of more highly reflective material visible. By the next sweep, the darker layer is gone and the asteroid itself is breaking apart."

"And it's headed our way? It can't possibly pose a danger to the ship. We passed that area days ago."

"Normally this would be true, but it seems that this moonlet is accelerating."

Samuels's jaw dropped. "What?"

"We have been bouncing radar off of it for hours now. It is accelerating. I think we can assume it began accelerating before we began to measure."

"What can do that?"

"Jupiter's gravitational influence?"

"No,." answered Xu.

"Wh-What are you saying?" The Doc stammered over comms from Blue Hab.

Cal looked to a cockpit camera and addressed her, "We're not going to say anything more than the facts. I'm sure we will speculate, but right now, let's stay focused on what we actually know."

All eyes on the ship returned to the images of the tiny moon. Except Cal's. He scanned the room and the faces on the screens, watching their expressions, waiting to see who would break the silence.

"Why didn't we pick up on this thing until now?" Samuels asked.

"We weren't looking behind us," Xu said.

"The ship's detection equipment is focused on keeping us from running into something," added Inez. "No one thought we'd need to worry about anything running into *us*."

"That seems like a design flaw," the pilot opined.

"We see it now, and it's catching up to us," said Cal.

"What do we do?"

"Run?" The Doc asked.

"We're not going to run," answered Cal.

"We don't have the fuel to run from it anyway, do we?"

"Propellant," Paul interjected.

"What?

"Not fuel. Propellant. There's a distinction where—"

"Paul," Cal cut off the engineer's tangent.

"Sorry. There's an important difference between the two, though."

Samuels spared him an annoyed look. "No, we don't really have the fuel to *run* per se, but we could burn to slingshot around Jupiter and back toward Earth if we wanted to."

"What would be the point of that? If this thing is hostile, we don't want to lead it back home, do we?"

"If it was hostile wouldn't it just have gone there in the first place?"

"Maybe not."

"Maybe it's spying on us and upset at being discovered?"

"It wasn't discovered," Cal pointed out. "We passed it by and never even noticed. It's revealed itself by coming after us, so detection doesn't seem to be a concern."

"You don't think it's from Ceres, do you?"

"Doubtful," said Xu. "They could have gotten something out here but they'd have to have anticipated our unexpected confrontation with them months ago. Given the way it all went down that seems unlikely to me."

In the space beyond the windows, Jupiter appeared to hang alone in the void.

"Maybe it's been spying on us *until* now?" Inez suggested.

"Yeah, maybe it's been watching us and—"

"And what?" Xu smiled. "It's been waiting to eat us?"

"Why not?" Asked the Doc, "We've got to consider every possibility, don't we?"

"Yes," Samuels said. "Like, what if it's a missile?"

"I just don't see how that would make sense. It's so monumentally difficult to reach another star, why would someone come all this way to do violence?"

"It's monumentally difficult for *us*. Maybe not for them."

"If it is a *them*," said Cal.

The Doc pursed her lips. "Why are we assuming it's from another star? What if it's some unprecedented form of life? What if this is a predator-prey thing?"

12

The module fell silent again.

"Maybe we've illegally entered the shrine of Olympus and this is the border patrol?"

Samuel's snickered.

"Don't laugh."

"Inez, please. Don't tell me you're really suggesting there has been some hidden Martian empire out here all along?"

"Martian?"

"She's trying to be dismissive," said Paul.

"Be dismissive, but is it just me or is that a powered object of unknown origin out there?"

"Potentially."

"Potentially?"

"Yes, potentially. We don't *know*. We could still be dealing with a natural phenomenon, or even false readings."

Cal took a deep breath and folded his arms over his chest. "All right, let's prepare to release a camera swarm. We need to get more data on this thing. We should be able to make better sense of it after getting a closer look."

"On it."

"In the meantime, we continue on course for Jupiter rendezvous and orbit. Now we just have an additional subject to study. I'm going to get on the line with control and hear what they have to say. I want all of you to put your heads together and come up with some procedures and contingencies for the approach of this thing."

"Yes sir!" they shouted. The Doc smiled out from a screen.

"We have two weeks of coasting until we need to start our braking burns, and there's an estimated ten days until this thing catches up to us. Is it likely that it will just fly by? What do we do if it invites us to dock? What do we do if it pops open and confetti shoots out? We just don't know what's ahead of us. We need to be ready for whatever may come." Cal looked around the interior of the module and across the faces on the screens. "Facing the unknown is the very essence of exploration. Let's try and imagine everything that we think could happen while it's still twenty-something million miles away from us. Let's be as prepared as we can."

"Doc?"

"Yes?"

"Start to think about the psychology of this. All of this. I'm talking about the potential for misunderstanding."

"I understand, Cal."

Xu, Inez and Samuels filed out of the command module, lining themselves up with the circular access port and propelling themselves down the ship's spinal corridor.

The pilot hesitated at the mouth of the port. "What if it *is* a missile?" she asked.

Cal gave her the side-eye. "Consider the possibility, Sarah. Come up with contingencies for it, but don't make that your default assumption. Please."

Six

From the outside, the *Ulysses* looked no different than press photos. Inside the vehicle was ablaze with unusual activity as the crew worked with control to come up with an unprecedented mission plan.

Ulysses loomed out of the darkness, a combination of flood and running lights formed a corona about the ship's surfaces. The centrifuge arms continued on their great swinging arcs, and giant multifaceted habitats hung out on the far ends of the Kapton-coated arms like the weights of a giant pendulum. Traveling down the spine, the stacked ring modules—the storage, computer and docking levels. Then the spindle, which ran through the carousel where the two hundred and fifty-foot-long automated tankers docked. Down past the tankers, the reactor and main engine ring culminated in a tangle of plumbing and the flaring of the main engine's exhaust bell. The electromagnetic field that deflected dust and helped intercept micrometeoroids was largely invisible save for a rare crackle of static along the field in front of the vessel.

The ship was filled with more activity than would have been expected at this point in the journey. The crew was anxious, burning more calories. Odysseus saw it reflected in the performance of the life-support systems and saw cause to change the ship's internal humidity and temperature settings. He passed the information along in his continuous report to the Doctor.

The Doctor herself floated into the docking ring. She preferred not to be alone in the sick bay while action took place. She was drawn to company. Besides, the engineer was always appreciative of her presence and insightful extra eye.

Paul Arthor was preparing to launch the camera swarm. The big engineer loaded a bottle-sized capsule of over one hundred and fifty polyhedron-shaped probes into a receptacle in the docking ring's wall. This receptacle was actually the smallest airlock in the module. He slid the capsule into a cylindrical device inside the tiny airlock, checked its alignment, and sealed the hatch. Arthor threw a lever and the cylinder shifted to emerge from an aperture on the ring's ventral side. It projected away from the ship on a telescoping armature. With the throw of a switch, a solenoid charged and threw the firing pin forward, igniting the explosive propellent in the bottom of the bottle-sized shell.

She watched out the window. Exactly like buckshot, one hundred and fifty disposable probes were blown out into the interplanetary spacecraft's wake. Firing the swarm of probes backwards out of the ship essentially slowed them down in comparison with the *Ulysses*. The ship quickly left them behind. The object behind them would pass through the swarm in a matter of days. The probes were without thrusters or guidance systems of any kind, but they had cameras on each of their polyhedral surfaces. They would sweep by the object and capture a storm of images before sailing off into space.

Nothing to do now but attend to their regularly planned duties and wait for time to pass. Rest and prepare.

Space travel was dominated by a lot of waiting around, the Doc thought. You could make your choice and then minutes, hours, days, or more would pass before you discovered if you'd made the right one or not. She marveled at how the flight crew handled such a disconnect between action and result. It took a special kind of person to adapt. She was on the mission, and theoretically, she could step into any other position in an emergency, but so much of spaceflight would always be alien to her way of thinking.

Xu Zuoren stood in front of one of the two large triangular windows on the spinward side of Red Hab. It was ironic that these windows should afford such an expansive view and yet the movement of the centrifuge rendered it a looping cacophony. It was only when the arms were spun down and retracted, the habitats locked to the hub, that those windows could be said to frame a real view. Now, the centrifuge spun and the view was akin to that from a merry-go-round. Xu enjoyed it nevertheless. It was a different perspective. What if there was a being who saw the world only in this way, as a whirling scan? He must suggest it to the Doctor, as much of their conversations had steered in that direction as of late.

He examined the latest data regarding the interloper on his screen. Out of the corner of his eye he caught a glimpse of orange and white, the spinning of the hab caused the Jovian to flash by the window. He had spent a decade studying and preparing for the mysteries of Jupiter and now . . . Now it had all been pushed to the back burner. Such was the magnitude of this discovery. His mind was as consumed by the new mystery as anyone's. Jupiter had been everything, and now it was almost nothing, and he rolled the strangeness of that around in his head. He should still have time to devote to Jupiter, but in relation to this discovery.
. .

What *was* it?

Why was it *here?*

Xu's quarters were a level "down," meaning further out toward the far end of the habitat. He enjoyed the officer's prerogative of the Mars-G sleeping quarters, and yet, he too was now having trouble falling asleep. It was not a result of listening to stories of his friend's condition, he was certain. He had never been susceptible to suggestion. He was having trouble sleeping for the same reason Cal was having trouble sleeping. It was a reaction to the extreme stress. He was, alas, a human being and it snuck out. When he spoke to the Doctor, he would have to inquire whether sleep issues had spread to other members of the crew.

Seven

The moon-thing was changing. As it approached the point in space where it would cease the application of thrust, it began shifting its internal structure. New avenues and channels for the application of force and movement of reaction mass formed within. Fractal whorls erupted across its surface—budding storms of geometric complexity erupted from the tips of the previous turbinations. A razor-fine stream of glittering dust sloughed off of the mushrooming structures and trailed away into space.

Eight

The camera swarm vanished. Cal caught a brief glimpse of them through a small rear-facing viewport in one of Red Hab's shorter side walls.

"How long till they reach the thing?" Cal turned to see Inez walk into the room, comfortable in the gravity of Red Hab's second floor. He was surprised he hadn't noticed her approach, but he knew whom it was before he turned his head.

"Sixteen hours and we should start seeing stuff better than what we can get with our telescope."

"And until then?"

"It gives us time to figure out the next step."

"Which is?"

"Well for you, the next step is to figure out how to communicate with it. For me, it's to try and figure out whether we should."

"You really think this thing might be . . . a *thing*?"

"It's possible. And if not, beaming messages at a speedy asteroid isn't going to hurt anybody."

"Whereas . . ."

"Yeah. Maybe. So, I need you tell me what those next steps are."

"I'm already going back and forth with control on the topic."

"Good."

"Fifteen different threads."

"Any consensus yet?"

"Kinda."

"Figure it out for me, Inez."

"I will. You make sure we should."

"I will."

Nine

The Doc wafted off the final rung of the ladder that led down from her quarters in Blue Hab. She'd just had her "morning" shower, and her hair was beginning to drift about her head in still damp curls. By the time she had finished the climb up and out of the habitat, and through two hundred and ninety-three-foot centrifuge arm to the hub, the gravity had diminished from Mars normal to zero. She pulled herself in through the hub and down to the storage ring, opening the padded door of a small locker to extract a gelatin bar.

The first images arriving from the swarm would be filtering in soon. Her copper hair bobbed wetly, and she shook it away from her face. This was getting to be a routine, she thought; gel-bar and popping in to the docking ring engineering station for important moments. She was getting too predictable. Maybe she should head up to the command module instead? She liked to give Cal his space, but it would be nice to be in the CM for the first close look at the moonlet. From this point on, until the camera swarm shot past it, the view would get better and better.

She tore the package open and held the candy-like nutrient bar between her teeth, pulling on strategically placed rungs, propelling herself toward the bow and up into the flared cone of the command module. Xu floated near the science station to port. Along the opposite wall, Inez had extracted a chair from beneath the comms/IT station and had strapped herself in. She wore headphones and had her eyes closed, listening. On her screens, windows filled with scrolling waveforms. She had one finger on the control panel, poised over the return key.

In the module's nose, the two command and piloting stations were occupied: the captain was strapped into the port couch, beneath the angular cockpit windows. Pilot Samuels, in casual clothes, was strapped into the starboard couch. Curving display panels looped over the seats and down between the two stations into a console of fail-safe physical gauges and a shared set of hand controllers.

The Doc floated into the nose and delivered a familiar squeeze on the shoulder to say hello to the pilot. This served to bring her to a bobbing halt in the darkened command pod. She turned to Cal. "Is that it?"

"Yes," he said.

A multitude of views of the moonlet were displayed on the screen in front of the captain. A half-completed 3D model of it was being constructed from the combined feed of the swarm cameras. It looked as if the asteroid was growing . . . tendrils? Feelers? Unscientific similes, she supposed, but how was one supposed to parse the absolute unknown? Was it possible to observe and not compare against life's experience? Instincts? Xu could, she was sure. Cal, sometimes. She could not. It reminded her that it had been a very long time since she had seen something truly *strange*.

This was *strange*.

The moonlet or asteroid fragment, or whatever it was now, appeared to be covered in, or possibly shedding, some form of growth. It curled off of its surface like ash-gray primordial ferns. There was something fundamental about the shape, like the curve of the nautilus. Ancient.

"It . . . changed, right? It wasn't like this before." She knew it wasn't.

"No, it wasn't." He knew she knew it wasn't, just as he knew she needed to hear him say it. He was going to need her counsel.

"Is it falling apart? Or is it growing?"

"Not sure yet. Could be both."

"Any recognizable surface features? Signs that maybe it's a vehicle or a probe of some kind?"

"Not that we have recognized as of yet, Doctor," Zuoren said from behind. "Nor have we seen visible signs of exhaust that might help explain the object's acceleration."

"Do we think it could be . . . alive?"

"You tell me, Doc," Cal said.

"Is that why you're glad I'm here?"

"That's not the only reason."

"Are there any openings in the surface at all?"

"None that we can see. The swarm was fired with a fairly tight dispersal pattern. We didn't want to risk putting any of them on a collision course, but as a consequence we're not going to be able to image its entire surface with this one swarm."

"Is it reacting to the cameras at all?"

"Again, not that we can tell."

"Unless those extrusions are somehow a response to the swarm." Cal opened another window on his display. "According to Xu, all that activity on the outer surface is producing a lot of waste heat, obscuring the signs of whatever process might be going on inside to power that thing."

"And it's not attempting to communicate?" The Doc looked at Cal and then over at Inez.

"Not that we can detect," the comms officer replied.

"Still gaining on us at the same rate?"

"Yes," Cal said.

"So, seven days till it gets here?"

"Yeah. You might want to use some of that time to figure out how we might tell if it's alive or not. And if it is, how such a being might perceive the universe."

"Tall order, but I'll do my best, Cal."

"Thanks, Susan."

"Thank *you*, I'm going to watch sci-fi movies for a week."

Ten

Cal shifted in the command seat and stared at an ever-updating flurry of images. The swarm was still hundreds of thousands of miles away from the object, but it was growing larger and clearer by the moment; each update revealed greater detail. The asteroidal fragment truly had become a shaggy *thing*. A ragged, shambling pursuer.

Despite himself, Cal felt a real visceral sense of fear, an ancient animal instinct toward the unknown. It was an earned fear. A wise, old fear. He did not dismiss it, but he refused to allow it to swamp him. He was sure the rest of the crew felt it as well, except maybe Xu, who was possibly an android. Cal smirked.

He typed a text message to the crew: *You are making history, but stay calm and let's all rise to the occasion.* He punctuated it with a video of the first moon landing. *Don't choke.*

As more fine details began to resolve, it appeared at times that the outer surface was moving over a deeper substrate. Underlying structures were glimpsed fleetingly, only to be covered again by a constant fractal wave that seemed to be endlessly remaking the moon.

Hours ticked by.

Eleven

Cal opened the door to his quarters and stepped in from the tiny hallway. He crossed to his loosely-made bunk and reached underneath. With the ripping sound of Velcro, he pulled out the silver briefcase he had taken from the Ceres rover and placed it on the blanket. The briefcase had a lock on it, like nothing else that he had encountered on the planetoid. A lock that was now broken. The silver case fell open, and he stared at the items inside: an ancient unmodified nickel-plated .357 magnum revolver, a red-striped cardboard box of bullets, and a custom-made translucent thermal jacket.

He picked the gun up out of its case and loaded it, listening to the fascinatingly subtle and frightening sound the bullets made as they slid into their chambers, and the finely machined tone of the cylinder as it nestled back into the frame. He pushed the revolver into the thermal sheath and returned it to the briefcase.

Twelve

"Now that we have a good baseline of images . . . I think we can move on and attempt . . . communication," Cal said. "Or at the very least we can see if there is any reaction to our transmissions."

The multipurpose antennae rose from the side of *Ulysses'*s flanks and extended away from the bulk of the ship.

"We're going to send a tight beam of messages directly toward the object." Inez reflexively stared out the viewports at the antennae in full extension, jutting from the ship.

"So, we're sure it's a vehicle? It's not an *it?* An animal?"

"We're not sure of anything."

"And we must keep in mind that communication might simply be impossible. We may not be able to discern its motives or intentions without a common frame of reference," Xu said.

Silence.

"Well . . ." Cal said and turned back to Inez. "Assuming it *is* possible. . ."

"Yes . . . assuming it's possible . . . all of the established guidelines for communication presuppose the receipt of a message from deep space. There just isn't a protocol for making first contact on the way to work."

"I'll be happy if we flash a light and they flash one back," Cal said.

"So, what's the plan?"

"We've gone back and forth with control and are in agreement on a process. Mostly." Inez shared her screen across ship, and a series of icons and windows spilled out of it.

"We've decided to use Odysseus to deliver a set of messages via a cycle of methods, trying to find some common basis of communication. Something that might elicit a reply. We will start with the mathematical, primes." She looked around at her compatriots. "Assuming that math is one of the common bases for understanding the universe, one of the first mysteries anyone would uncover are the prime numbers. Hopefully, a demonstration of this commonality of understanding will be recognized. Failing a response, we will follow with scientific messages beginning with a binary description of the hydrogen atom and then using that as a basis for encoding pictorial messages—a bitmap vocabulary of symbols representing numbers and mathematical operations."

"Radio?"

"Yes, multiple transmission methods along the EM spectrum. Infrared, radio, microwave, light-pulse, and maybe laser."

"Sounds good."

"How about computational communication?" Arthor asked.

"Control was pretty adamant about algorithmic being our attempt of last resort."

"Why's that?" Arthor asked.

Zuoren replied, "For one thing, the benefits of the methodology are more profound if the communication is over very long distances, but there's also a great deal of concern over the unintended consequences that could result from describing a self-propagating virtual machine to another species. There is the fear that it could be interpreted as an act of aggression."

"No argument here. I won't even open messages from my parents."

Thirteen

"Nothing?"

Cal floated just over the shoulder of Inez's seat along the curving starboard wall of the command module. She had her own lab with capabilities that duplicated and expanded upon those in the CM, but for moments like this there was no substitute for the synergy of talented people working together in the same space. She had hoped they would have been working in concert by now, solving mysteries together as history opened its arms and secrets were revealed, but nothing was happening at all. There was no response to their attempts at communication. No matter what transmission type or communications methodology they employed there was no response. Or no *discernible* response.

"We tried flashing our lights. No one flashed back."

"Have we tried actually flashing our lights?" the Doc asked.

"Yes, we have literally tried flashing our lights. No response."

Paul spoke up, "This is going to sound silly, but how about waving at it with the manipulator arm?"

Laughter.

"No, hear me out. I said it would sound silly, but the thing is growing arms and tendrils all over itself, and they're waving around constantly, right? Maybe physical motion might elicit a physical response?"

They all looked around at one another.

A few minutes later, the ship's giant arm lifted away from its moorings and did a fair approximation of a big friendly wave. A slight back and forth movement at the shoulder joint, greater range at the elbow, more quickly at the wrist.

They watched via the ship's telescopes.

Hours ticked away.

Nothing.

Fourteen

The camera swarm swept past the asteroidal moon. The probes would continue to transmit until their batteries wore down, but *Ulysses* had already stopped listening. The swarm vanished into space.

The former moon's behavior remained unaltered.

Its outer surface continued to convulse, an external wave that crested at its tail. Tendrils and filamentary structures rose only to collapse back into the structure as fractal foam.

"Fascinating, isn't it," Xu asked rhetorically. Maybe. "It has been in a state of continuous change since we first started observing it. Our understanding of it has hardly altered although it clearly has exhaust from an engine of some kind that must be powering its acceleration."

"At least we know that much," Cal said.

"Does that mean it's a ship?"

"Not necessarily."

"The propagation of the surface patterns might relate to an internal mechanism of propulsion. Whether that mechanism is a natural one or the construction of intelligence I can't say."

"The movement on the surface might be connected to the exhaust trail—expelled reaction mass or the waste products of some form of combustion? Maybe ejection of some fraction of its own mass for propulsion," said Cal.

"It's as good a theory as any."

"Repeat the communications attempt."

Nothing.

The hours ticked away.

Fifteen

When the final images from the swarm were integrated into the database, the changes shown in the time-lapse flyby were bewildering. The moonlet indeed seemed to be remaking itself. Whirling Mandelbrot sets of complexity congealed into new tendrils and armatures, reaching ahead as if the very structure of the object was exuding itself forward; disassembling from the stern and rebuilding at the bow as if to somehow hasten its arrival.

"What the hell is it?" Cal accidentally spoke aloud. What could it possibly be doing? What should *he* be doing? They had the responsibility of history in front of them, but he had a responsibility to his ship, to keep the situation under control. How could one approach a moment such as this with an open heart while still guarding one's nuts? He felt as if he were leaving them wide open.

He scrolled back to the beginning of the time-lapse and admired images of his ship caught by the departing swarm. *Ulysses* was the most advanced vessel that humanity had ever devoted to science and exploration. It was able to survive the hostile environment of deep space, capable of shielding itself against micrometeoroids and the blazing radiation of the Jovian planets. And it was fast, if the planets were in proper phase the ship could travel from the Earth to Mars in only thirty days, its top speed limited only by the amount of fuel it could carry. But in this unexpected encounter, Cal was terribly cognizant of how vulnerable the giant spacecraft could be.

"Is it an *it*? Or is it a vessel?" he asked his resident scientist.

"There is just not enough evidence to say anything more from what we've thus observed."

"I understand, but this isn't a damn peer review, Xu. This is *happening*. Tell me what your gut says. What is this thing?"

"This is just speculation, you understand."

"I get it."

"All right. My best . . ." He surveyed the faces in the module's interior. "My best guess, given what we have seen, is that this is a probe. Possibly sent from another star as just a few grams worth of molecular machine, designed to transport the bulk of its body as weightless information. Completing itself only after it had reached its target."

"That would certainly make interstellar travel easier."

"So, the asteroid . . ."

"Was consumed as raw material, yes. For propulsion and transformation."

Cal pulled at his chin. "So . . . what is it transforming into?"

"What we see before us."

"Which is?"

"I have no idea. Perhaps it isn't finished building itself yet . . . or is in transition to a new form."

"Maybe it's already what it needs itself to be?" Inez suggested.

"Maybe. Or maybe it's malfunctioning."

"We just don't know."

"The most important thing to keep in mind *is* how much we don't know. This is simply a unique moment in human history." Cal let that statement settle for a moment. It was a message far larger than the messenger; he realized the gravity of the words only as they had left his mouth.

"And to complicate matters, we have no actual procedure to follow."

"You mentioned," the Doc said.

"There are protocols for finding microbes, and there are protocols for receiving transmissions from deep space, but the universe is so mind-bogglingly large, and therefore the chances of face-to-face contact were so small, that the only protocols ever written about physical contact away from the Earth were written in the '50s."

That's not so old." Inez piped.

"1950s."

"Oh."

"So, what do we do?"

"I say we come up with our own plan. Control will too, obviously. So, we will take what we like from their plan, add it to ours, and then probably throw all of it out when that thing gets here."

Sixteen

The big engineer opened the hatch in the docking ring's floor and dropped into the cramped spindle corridor, heading aft toward the engine and reactor complex. He needed to check the tank pressures. Though he could get those readings from anywhere within the ship on his phone or any number of tablets or personal screens, with events rushing toward them, Paul Arthor felt the need to check the physical gauges themselves. To see them with his own eyes.

It was an itch. Nerves.

The plumbing and piping of the main engine ran throughout the spindle and the four-story engineering ring, but all the gauges were arrayed together in a windowed console on the second floor.

It took him a few minutes to leisurely fall through the corridor and land gently on the other side. He swung open the hatch and was greeted by the sight of the top of the reactor tower and the engine beyond. The floors of the engineering ring encircled the tower, providing three-hundred-and-sixty-degree access. He passed through the red and blue grated partitions, stood before the valves, and began to compare their values to his electronic readings.

His nerves settled as he confirmed each number. He looked back up the way he came. The tower was crowned with incoming and outgoing pipes and thick electrical cables that ran off in every direction, feeding the various systems of the ship. The ship that cradled and nurtured their fragile little bodies.

Out beyond the tubes, cables, and conduits, beyond the thin skin of the ship, was the *thing*. And it was close.

Seventeen

It happened just like docking a tanker but on a larger scale. At the limits of visual detection, the object slid out of the void. It was only a fraction of the size it had been as part of the binary asteroid, but it was still colossal, nearly *Ulysses*'s length and over twice its width. And it was a horror, a discus shape hidden beneath a tendril-decked surface that waved and undulated like a kelp forest assaulted by waves. In just moments, its perceived diameter eclipsed the size of the ship's engine bell.

Cal looked over his shoulder into the rear section of the CM and caught Inez's eye. She shook her head—still no response to any of their attempts at communication. He reported the lack of contact, again, to control. They'd get the message in another thirty-eight minutes. By the time any response could get back to the ship, the thing would be upon them. He opened the channel again and added, "It seems intent on making a close approach to the *Ulysses*. I am made uncomfortable by these events but believe it is my duty to maximize our chances for a positive first contact, as such I am taking no further action at this time." He sent the Quindar tone that closed the transmission.

On the screens, the alien loomed larger.

"All right, Paul." Paul Arthor appeared on his screen. "Retract and lock the habitats."

In Blue Hab, the Doc gathered her tablet and coffee pod and moved to the ladder in the center of the room. When the habitat retracted, elements of the material that made up the arm would fold into its top floor, turning the spacious cafeteria into a tight vestibule. She climbed up to the second floor, into her sick bay office, as the cafeteria's tables and chairs sank into the floor much in the way an origami swan might be unfolded into a piece of paper.

In the docking ring, Paul pushed himself along the curved engineering workstation and threw a physical switch. The centrifuge slowed and stopped. The two hundred and ninety-foot long bronzed arms began to deflate and collapse, accordion-style, as the habitats were drawn in toward the centrifuge hub. Each habitat secured itself to the hub via massive clamps, sending a slight shudder down the ship's long axis. Arthor glanced at the indicators; Red Hab and Blue Hab both read locked. The ship was presenting its smallest profile in case of collision or other emergency.

Cal observed from the command module as the ship furled its habitats. The rearview image floated in his HUD; with the arms out of the way, the alien dominated the sky behind the ship. An unbidden visual illusion was forming, a sense of being trapped between the hammer of Jupiter's pale orange sphere and the ragged anvil of the shape arriving behind them. It appeared to slide off to the left of *Ulysses*'s engine bell, growing larger by the second. It should pass by a few hundred meters off their starboard side.

If there's anyone to talk to, who should be the first to try? To try and meet them? The questions rang in his head. *The captain, of course.* Cal wondered whether or not that should be a given. *Me? Is there someone else in the crew that might be better?*

Nah.

"Odysseus, I want you to automatically continue the communication attempts. Once one attempt is finished, repeat it immediately."

Cal floated out of his command seat and snatched his helmet off the back of his chair with a gloved hand. "Crew of the spaceship *Ulysses*, docking maneuvers-protocol, please. Full suits, helmets at the ready." He wanted to remember the moment and scanned the room. Samuels was strapped into the right-hand command seat. Inez floated at her comms station and across the module. Xu bobbed in front of his science station, folding its screens flush. "Assume this is going to be a face to face meeting. Historic. The biggest moment in the history of space exploration. Ever." He stopped. Eyes stared at him in the instrument-lit module. "I don't want to oversell it, judge for yourself."

The object would make its closest approach, assuming it didn't match orbits with them, within minutes.

"Xu, Inez, you're with me. Sarah—" He looked at his pilot and knew he need say nothing. She slid over to his vacated left-hand seat. He tabbed open his comm line. "Doc, I have to get something from my quarters. Meet me in the docking ring if you're not already there."

Eighteen

By the time Cal reached the docking ring, the alien dominated the circular sweep of viewports. Xu and Inez floated just ahead of him in their red and yellow suits, marveling at the sight. Cal placed the silver briefcase against the Velcro patch on a counter just inwards of the hatch. Rippling points of starfire light could be seen erupting all over its forward edge. Incandescent matter was being propelled forward into its direction of travel.

Cal opened his comm line to the CM. "Sarah, are you seeing this?"

"Yeah."

"It's slowing down."

"Yes. What do we do?"

"Nothing right now, but keep the thrusters hot, prime the main. Be ready to move."

"Got it."

The object slid to a relative halt half a mile off the *Ulysses's* starboard side. Zuoren, still attempting to discern a relationship between the alien and the gas giant, noted that this meant that they were each now following a similar orbit toward a rendezvous with Jupiter.

As it's motion slowed, the willowy fronds and spiraling tendrils thrashed in rippling cascades of frantic activity.

"What's going on with it? It seems agitated."

"Indeed."

"Looks that way to me too, Cal, but we have to remember our own bias. Bias that arises from our shared fundamental experience as human beings. Our visitor isn't going to share that bias," said the Doc.

"Unless it's just an animal."

So energetic was the motion that some of the larger tendrils exuded their own distal tips, which instantly lost color and dissociated into sprays of ash drifting around the former moonlet.

"What should we do?"

"Maybe we go out to meet them?"

"In the lander?"

"No, I think one of us should go out there."

"You're joking."

"I'm not. One of us should go out there. Stand on the surface of our ship. Let them know that there are beings inside and answer the questions we have about them about us. . . for them. If you know what I'm trying to say."

"I think so."

"Normally, I'm quite eloquent."

"You are, but this is a helluva time for that talent to desert you."

Cal placed the helmet bowl over his head, slid it into the groove on the suit's neck ring, and twisted. The ring sealed and the helmet's HUD lit up. He moved to the Extra Vehicular Activity airlock. From inside the docking ring, it looked no different than the ports reserved for pressurized craft. From the outside, the EVA lock bulged to house an inner vestibule capable of accommodating two suited astronauts and their gear.

"Okay, open ship-wide comms. Sarah, be ready."

"Roger."

"Xu, Doc, I'll want your thoughts."

They nodded.

"Inez, watch for responses of any kind along every spectrum of measurement you can think of. Keep me in the know."

"You got it, Cal."

"And, Paul, stand by that airlock and get me inside quick if things go sideways."

"As quickly as is possible."

"Please."

Cal entered the airlock and sealed the door behind him. Arthor gave him a thumbs up through the interior viewport. He turned to face the airlock's outer door; warning lights strobed red on all four corners. There was a brief puff of escaping gas and glittering dust, and the door swung outwards.

Nineteen

Cal rounded the exterior of the docking ring, and the object appeared like a vast sunrise in his faceplate. He stopped and attached a tether to a safety rail ahead, and then pivoted to disconnect another from the end of the rail behind, before continuing on. He stood and resumed his climb around *Ulysses*'s waistline. In the crystalline emptiness, the detail visible on the alien was staggering even though it was still a half-mile away. Tendrils pulsed and convulsed while the shadows of considerable movement could be detected within. As if mass was being shifted up through the tendrils to fuel their growth.

His boots snugged up firmly against the skin of the ship, adhering through the aluminum skin to the layers of piping and steel strut work beneath. He stood and stared into the first truly alien vista any human had ever witnessed.

Across a lake of nothingness was an island of recursive complexity. The thing was reaching out in every direction at once, fractal appendages waxing and waning as if steadying itself in space. He didn't know what else to do; he waved.

"Are you guys getting this?"

Mid-wave he reached over and tapped the suit-screen on his left forearm. Brilliant points of light came on at his fingertips. The glove lights were designed for working in the oppressive darkness of the shadows of space, like the craters of the moon or out here in the depths where the sun was only a bright pinprick. Ironically, they were found to be most useful in reviewing mission tapes and determining exactly how someone screwed up.

Cal's waves became arcs of starlight.

"Yes. Incredible view, Cal."

"Did you see me waving at it?"

"Yes. You looked silly."

"I was afraid of that."

"We're recording all this for posterity, Cal. Don't curse."

"No promises." He looked around him; the object seemed to be getting larger.

A Quindar tone sounded. "It's on the move," Samuels said.

"I thought so," Cal said. "Coming toward us?"

"Yes, three point six miles per hour."

"Move us away, I'm tethered so don't worry about me."

There was a blast from thrusters all down the length of the ship.

"Roger."

The tether went taut, and Cal's legs bounced against the ship's skin. *Ulysses* retreated from its pursuer.

"Is it still coming?"

"Yes, it is."

"Change the plane of motion, Sarah."

"Roger," she said and rotated a luminous dial on the ship's control UI. Every thruster along the spine of the *Ulysses* fired in a burn that sank the interplanetary ship diagonally away from the former moonlet.

"Let's see what it does," Cal said.

Four bright lights flared on the far side of the object and immediately the distance between it and *Ulysses* began to shrink more rapidly.

"Well, we finally got a response!" Inez shouted.

46

"Running away elicited a response. Is that a good sign?"

"Doesn't seem like a good sign."

"Sarah!" Cal shouted into his helmet mic.

"It's coming in quicker, but I can maintain the distance between us at 20 percent thrusters."

"Do it."

"Roger, but I don't recommend it for long. It's going to eat up some fuel."

"Noted."

Cal stood as straight as he could, turned on the high-powered light in his hand, and waved. "How do I look?"

"Conspicuous."

"Good."

"Heroic?"

"Oh yes."

"It's increasing its speed toward us. I'm up to 23 percent and climbing to maintain the distance."

"Maybe you're just irresistible, Cal?"

"Are we *sure* it's not a missile?" Sarah asked, voice crackling over his helmet speakers.

"No, we are not, but missiles don't usually engage their targets so slowly."

"Cold comfort."

What the hell does it want? Cal's mind swirled. *It won't respond to any form of communication. And it won't take no for an answer. What if it is some kind of space-going animal and this is predator-prey behavior?*

He waved both hands far over his head. *C'mon you damn* thing. Things? *I'm doing everything I can possibly think of!*

"Maybe it *is* a missile."

"Odysseus, prep and launch the lander. Bring it around and position it between us and the alien."

"Good idea, Captain," Xu said.

The lander was already rising up over the side of the ship. Far heavier than the taxi landers used in most applications, the *Ulysses* lander was built for exploration and carried a larger descent stage, exploration tools, a greater quantity of consumables, and an impressive amount of general illumination and searchlights. It pirouetted as it rose over the curve of the docking ring.

"Maintaining roughly one quarter-mile distance, thrusters up to 26 percent."

"We won't need to keep this up for long. The lander's almost in position."

The hulking bug-like vehicle passed over Cal's head and sailed into the intervening space. It rotated as its thrusters fired to position itself between the alien and the *Ulysses*.

"Turn the lights on," Cal said.

Bright beams erupted from the lander's descent lights and spotlights as it turned to face the object.

"All right. Sarah, ease off the thrusters. Odysseus, keep the lander between that thing and the *Ulysses*."

"Are you coming back in, Cal?"

"I probably should."

"Does that mean you're not?"

"Yeah. Not quite yet."

"You have something planned you want to clue me in on?"

"No, this is just a helluva view."

"Rub it in."

The alien closed in on the *Ulysses*. Tendrils and swirling fronds swept across its surface, concentric rings of activity pulsing on the side nearest the Earth ship.

Twenty

From his vantage point on the surface of the ring, Cal watched the known meet the unknown. A skyscraper-sized ziggurat of swirling fractal shapes erupted in slow motion from the alien's leading surface. It reached out toward the lander and swept it gently aside. Odysseus fought against the action with rapid-fire bursts from the lander's thrusters and its articulated main engines. Wherever the fractally regenerating structure came into contact with the lander, it gave way as if some force holding it together was suddenly withdrawn. Huge chunks tumbled and collapsed while self-symmetric debris showered off into space and rained down over the *Ulysses*'s starboard side.

Cal reflexively shielded his face as a fan of debris washed over him. The pelting of the fractal ash against his spacesuit sounded and felt like being hit with a spray of snow. He examined a line of debris drifting off the blue material of his suit; it even looked like snow. Crystalline, gear-like, melting away.

He turned his attention back to the lander. The monstrous arm may have been disintegrating but much of the force of its movement was still delivered to the lander, which was being gently but firmly shoved away. It bobbled around the side of the object and was pushed off by the cilia-like movements of structures erupting across the surface.

Cal began running in leaps across the skin of the docking ring, dragging the tether along the rail.

"I'm on my way back in!"

As soon as the lander had been cleared from the area, the alien closed the remaining distance between the two space vehicles. Orifices opened on its surface and thruster flame belched outwards to avoid a collision. In an impressive display of either conspicuous fuel usage or advanced propulsion technology, the former moonlet positioned itself directly astride the Earth ship. Geometric towers cascaded from the strange surface, generated in a furiously churning mass of material, growing out toward the *Ulysses* with horrifying speed. Heat from the activity swamped the ship's infrared detectors.

Cal scrambled along outside the ring. Those towers would bridge the remaining distance, making contact with the ship's hull in equidistant points around the EVA airlock. His airlock.

"It's coming!"

"What!"

Cal unhooked his tether and slid across the curved surface under the alien construction points bubbling toward the airlock. "It's hooking up to the docking ring. Dropping a connecting tunnel or something directly over the EVA airlock." A skin was forming between each of the alien towers, a tunnel growing down toward *Ulysses*'s hull. "I'm going to try to get in ahead of it."

"Is that wise?"

"You tell me. Do you want to empty the ring of atmosphere so I can come in one of the lander ports? I'd rather not. I don't want to take my eyes off it."

"Can you make it in time?"

Cal slid across the curving surface, bringing the magnetic soles of his boots down against the skin as he neared the airlock. His feet slid to a stop, but his body twisted around, and he felt a sharp pain in his left knee. Glancing upwards, he became disoriented; it looked as if he was staring down into a mineshaft bored deep into stratified rock.

"I'm here." He pushed down on the outer airlock handle and squeezed the backpack of his suit in past the hatch, closing it quickly and slamming the lock closed. The warning lights flashed blue. He could feel the fabric of his suit press in toward him, the bubble dome helmet creaked. Pressure had returned to the lock. The inner door opened and Calvin Scott spilled out into the docking ring.

Arthor caught him and pivoted him upright. The Doc touched her helmet to his and looked him in the eyes. "You okay?"

"Yeah."

She checked his suit's onboard health status against the digital indicators. They matched. She checked his pupils through the helmet.

"You look good to me, too." She returned the medical readout screen to her hip.

Beyond Xu's red-suited form, Cal saw a shadow fall across the airlock viewport. The tunnel had been completed.

"It's a boarding tunnel. I got in just in time."

"Are you sure it's a *boarding* tunnel?"

"No. I don't know, but it made or grew *some* kind of tunnel. It must have a reason. And it grew quickly. Like watching wax melt."

"We've seen."

"Maybe it's a mouth?"

Xu shot Paul a look.

"That's disturbing," the Doc said.

Cal jumped. "There might be some on my suit!"

"What?"

"Debris. It landed on me, touched my suit."

"Contamination? I hope not."

"Good thing we all kept our helmets on."

The Doctor quickly grabbed a strip of clear tape from her bag and stretched it across the arm of his suit and pulled back. She held it up to the light. "Inez?"

"Yes?"

"Turn on your magnifier and let's get a quick look."

Inez took out her ship-phone and held it up to the strip.

"Pretty clean."

The Doc craned over Inez's phone. "Just looks like a little standard issue dust. Quarantine procedures need to enter into our thinking more. My fault."

Cal sat up. *What's it doing?*

Xu' s red suit was at the inner airlock window. The tunnel had solidified into a structure that was paper thin yet appeared as if it were made of stone. It exhibited no sign of the activity that played out over the surface of the object itself.

"What are we going to do now? Punch it with the manipulator?" Arthor asked.

"Maybe we should?"

Cal got to his feet and pushed himself over to the airlock, next to his mission scientist. Their helmets clinked together as they stared out through the two sealed airlock doors and into the blackness of the solidified shaft beyond. "I guess this is where we meet face to face?"

"I don't see that we have a choice."

"So, what do we do now?"

"Maybe we should figure out if this is a meeting or an invasion before we do anything?"

"I'm inclined to agree, but how do we do that? How do we control the pace of this contact?"

"I don't know, but I'm working on it."

"At least they are not overly hostile."

"They aren't?" The Doc's surprise was genuine.

"No. They could easily have destroyed us, collided with us. They took care not to damage the lander," Xu said.

"So, what? Maybe they're just grabby?"

Cal rose to one knee. "We're going to find out." He finished standing, and continued, "Inez, get on the horn and transmit a report of the situation thus far back to control."

"Roger." Inez bobbed away to the far side of the ring and spoke softly into her phone.

Cal turned to Xu and opened his mic. "We need to take stock of this situation."

"They have made no attempts to breach the outer airlock door, which a hostile force would surely attempt to do."

"Do we know that?"

"There doesn't seem to be any sign of intrusion from the interior anyway."

"Odysseus, the lander's cameras. Please position the vehicle to give us an exterior view."

"Yes, sir." On every screen in the ring, a window opened to show the view from the lander as it repositioned itself. The outer airlock door was completely obscured. The "boarding tunnel" was a slate gray polyhedral shape. Inert. It looked more a natural part of the *Ulysses* than it did the seething mass of the alien.

"How about we open the outer door?" asked Cal.

"Let them in the airlock vestibule?"

"If it's a *them*."

"That's an awful lot to ask; please step into this small enclosed space. If I were them, I'd worry that it could just as easily be a prison cell as an invitation to visit."

"Possibly, although they might not have the same concept of individuality that we do."

"All I know is that I'd rather invite them into ours than deal with the uncertainty of being invited into theirs," said the Doc.

"Open the outer airlock door."

Arthor rotated the glowing disc on his interface, and the outer airlock door swung open. The lights in the airlock chamber remained red, confirming the readings Paul was getting on his tablet. Although open to the interior of the tunnel, there was no atmosphere or pressure within the brightly lit airlock vestibule.

In the command module, the pilot seethed. Who would have ever thought that the pilot's position would be the consolation prize in space exploration's greatest moment? The panoramic cockpit windows afforded a beautiful view of the approaching Jovian system, but to watch the encounter with the object-moonlet-*thing* she had to resort to a screen. Which she, of course, had.

Cal again examined the blue-striped arm of his spacesuit, looking for any trace of the alien snowflakes. There was none.

The vestibule was still empty, outer door still open. Spilled light illuminated a rock-like shaft beyond the outer airlock door that quickly vanished into darkness.

"Maybe no one's coming?"

"An automated ship?"

"Can we get a drone in there?"

"There are drones in the lockers, but we can't get any in there without opening the inner door."

"We should have thought of that first."

"All right, let's close the outer door and then—"

Cal and Zuoren both involuntarily jumped backwards and away from the airlock viewport. A torrent of what looked like red-black liquid flooded into the atmosphere-less airlock.

Cal stumbled backwards but was steadied by the Doc as she crowded behind them to see. The fluid poured like an oil spill and billowed out as it hit the chamber floor, rising up in waves that crashed against the walls and fell back again and again. The airlock began to fill. As the waves crested and rose over the viewport it was clear that the liquid was no such thing. It was a very fine grain powder colored so darkly red that it appeared black in all but its highlights.

"Close the outer door!"

"Wait!" Zuoren shouted.

"Are you kidding?"

"No! What if this *fluid* is a being and it's only partially through the doorway? We might kill it."

"Maybe it should have thought of that before . . . *pouring* in unannounced?"

"We've been trusting so far, why stop now?"

"Why? Maybe because a giant blood waterfall just jumped into my airlock?"

"To *you* it looks like blood, to *them* I'm sure it looks like something different."

"Cal, let me through," the Doctor interrupted, shouldering her forest green spacesuit between the two of them and holding her medical screen up to the airlock window. It magnified and focused on the individual granular elements of the "fluid." The mass was growing filamentary processes as it moved. A deeper magnification revealed the fractal structure plain as day, as new growths of the searching, curling elements interleaved. Shifting, changing, restructuring themselves as they swept along with the fluidic motion.

"*Look* at that!" she said. "Is it a machine?"

"Very possible," Zuoren said. "Individual machines that small might be able to draw on power stored in the wavelike motion of the mass itself and work together to achieve greater and greater function."

"So that . . . material is one of *them*?"

"One of the crew?"

"Possibly. I thought you said it was a probe?"

"Maybe it's the entire crew?"

"Maybe it's not. Maybe this is a fuel tanker and it thinks we're a gas tank?"

"Close the outer door. Now."

"Right, boss." Arthor stabbed at the switch. The exterior airlock door swung inwards from the maw of the alien tunnel and closed, latch cycling. The flow was cut off cleanly by the closing door.

Three helmets, blue, green, and red crowded the airlock window. The granular fluid was not adhering to the walls or floor. In the absence of gravity, it had accumulated into a globular shape filling about half of the space of the vestibule.

"What in God's name is going on?"

"We opened our door, and it came in."

"So, we play host?"

"We try again to communicate. This time in person."

"Does it expect us to open the door, you think?"

"I'm not going to open the door. At least not yet."

Cal stepped in close to the airlock and put his gloved palm flat against the viewport.

Nothing happened. He held his hand there, staring at the strange globular mass, expecting a pseudopod to strike out at the transparent material and touch or otherwise approximate his gesture.

Nothing happened.

Cal retreated, floating back into line with Xu and the Doc. "What do you think?" Inez and Arthor edged in closer.

"Don't open the door," said the Doc.

"I do believe we need to continue to make overtures," Xu said. "We've tried radio, infrared, laser, your various attempts at waving."

Cal half-smiled. "What else are we supposed to do? I'm not letting that . . . in here."

Arthor, captivated by the dark red globular mass, leaned in closer to the window. "This looks weird."

"Now what?"

"Its border has gotten fuzzy. Its fuzzy."

The Doctor placed her med screen up against the glass.

"It's growing."

Cal leaned in to look at the magnification on her screen. Dark red but otherwise perfect miniature replicas of the shapes on the moonlet were expanding out from the surface of the globule.

"Quickly."

Looking away from the magnification, the thing's surface was visibly differentiating. The whorls and spirals were becoming distinct at a larger scale.

"Tell me why we shouldn't blow it out the airlock."

"We can't do that."

"Yes, we can."

"We *invited* it here."

"Only after it pursued and grabbed hold of us. Blow it out the airlock, Cal."

"What if it's . . . some kind of ambassador and is in the process of transforming itself to survive in our environment?"

"If it was an ambassador, it would have talked to us by now. If something had invaded our bodies like this, you'd have me cut it out. Without delay."

"I agree, this feels more like an infection than a visitation."

Xu looked pained; he was at a loss to try and defend his desire to refrain from ejecting the substance.

"I say we get that thing out the airlock."

"And just how are we going to do that?"

"That's easy," Arthor said. "Repressurize the vestibule, and then open the outer door. The escaping atmosphere should shoot the thing right back up the tunnel."

Cal weighed the mood and opinion of his crew, contemplating the future a heartbeat at a time.

"The tunnel's gone," Inez suddenly exclaimed.

"What?"

"I just looked up and it was gone!"

They all turned to look up and out the viewports; the tunnel had indeed vanished. The nearer end had fractured into drifting ash, the portions of the towers nearer to the source were collapsing upwards and sinking back into the alien's mass. Cal propelled himself to the topmost viewport. The instant the towers were subsumed, all surface activity ceased. The quiescent moonlet began to heel over, rotating on its long axis and drifting slowly toward *Ulysses*'s tail.

"What *is* going on?"

"I don't know, Cal."

"Is it going to hit us?"

"I . . . don't think so."

"Odysseus?"

"No, the object's motion does not indicate collision danger at this time."

"I can't see *anything* from up here," Samuels groused from the cockpit. "As usual."

"Odysseus, I want you to keep an eye on that thing. We should have been notified the instant the tunnel began to break up."

"Yes, Captain. Sorry, Captain."

"Sarah, I want you to keep your eye on that thing as well. It's your department for the time being."

"Roger."

Xu was back at the inner airlock door. "The filaments are growing larger."

Cal floated over, the Doctor trailing close behind. Churning fractal growth was generating red-black spirals that corkscrewed toward the inner surfaces of the airlock. It *was* as if wax were melting sideways. His attention felt impossibly split between multiplying potential emergencies. Tendrils had already grown to make contact with the plastic skin of the walls, doorframe, the inner door.

"I think it's attached itself."

"So much for getting it out of the airlock."

"I'm getting tired of hearing myself say *now what?* We need to get ahead of this thing."

"I don't know how to get ahead of something like this. How do we do anything but react?"

"We *could* have blown it out the airlock."

Alarms started to flash. "Cabin pressure drop," Odysseus announced.

"Everyone's helmets are sealed, yes?"

"Yes."

"Yessir."

"Yeah."

The Doc, directly in Cal's line of sight, just nodded.

"A leak?"

"Negative. It is not a continuous drop. Pressure loss consistent with airlock vestibule volume," said the AI.

"The inner door seal has failed!"

"What about the outer door?"

"If the outer seal had also failed, we'd still be losing atmosphere."

Xu pointed into the vestibule. "The fluid hasn't spread toward the outer airlock door at all; if it is responsible for the compromised seal, this is good news."

"Where's the breach?"

Arthor was closely examining the seal with a flashlight built into the finger of his suit.

"Odysseus?"

"Cabin pressure stable, Captain."

Cal turned to Paul Arthor. "Do you see anything?"

"Not yet."

The Doctor pushed off the floor and drifted upwards. She pulled herself along the donut ceiling toward the airlock's doorframe. "Here."

There were red-black tendrils, creeping like a tubular mold, projecting along the wall from the doorframe.

Cal pushed out into the middle of the docking ring. A zero-G space, the ceiling and floor were grates projecting from a window studded torus that tapered into the wide circular corridor running through the spine of the ship. The stations and docking ports around the walls were surrounded with blinking status lights. All except the EVA airlock. All of its lights had gone out.

"Here too," Arthor said. "Tips of tendrils coming through between the door and the frame."

"I don't like this one bit." Cal looked at his engineer. "Paul, lock off the access to the spindle. Close every door between here and the reactor complex. Inez, you do the same thing with the rest of the ship. Close the airtight doors between docking and the storage ring. Seal the doors between storage and lab ring as well and close off the CM. We have to find out if we can stop this thing, but in the meantime, I want to slow it down as much as possible. Throw up every physical barrier you can think of."

Cal turned to Xu and the Doc. "We are going to evacuate this ring for the time being. Don't worry, Xu. I'm not giving up on communication. but we need to know what we're dealing with. Try and get a sample of these tendrils and then get to the lab."

He flew "down" to the hatchway that lead aft to the spindle. Paul Arthor was squeezing his tool bag into the tunnel.

"Paul." Cal put a gloved hand onto the hatch cover. "You might be cut off down there for a while, are you sure you don't want to close from the stern up and then come forward with the rest of us?"

"No, that would take too long. We should cut the docking ring off sooner rather than later. At least until we see how fast this thing is spreading."

"We are going to need your help with this thing."

"I can assist from the engineering ring, and Xu and Inez will be up front. But if we're cut off and need someone at this end of the ship and I'm not here . . ."

"Point taken." He squeezed the bigger man's shoulder. "While you're locking things up down there, I need you to start working on stopping it."

"How? We know literally nothing about it."

"Xu and the Doc are on it. They'll get us something we can use. In

60

the meantime, just use your imagination."

"It's coming through!"

Cal closed the hatch and pushed off toward the other side of the ring, heading for the hatchway into storage. He grabbed at a safety railing and angled himself toward the activity at the EVA airlock. "What's happening?"

Xu turned in his red suit. "The tendrils are spreading across the wall but every time we cut one it just falls to ash beyond the slice." He turned back to assist the Doctor, placing a lid over a plastic container.

"Almost done. Getting samples." The Doc shook her glove, and the cutting tool she'd used drifted out of her hand.

"Leave it," she said.

They pushed away from the floor and bounced off the ceiling, heading through the hatch and up the corridor one by one. Cal pitched his silver briefcase in first, turned a somersault, and dropped into the corridor, pulling the hatch closed behind him.

Twenty-One

"What is going on down there? What's that stuff in the airlock!" Samuels queried as Inez propelled herself into the command module and shifted her orientation to align with the door controls. The hatch to the CM had never been closed in Samuels's entire time as *Ulysses* pilot, except during drills, but there was Inez pulling the straps off the tie-downs and getting ready to slide it shut.

"We're being invaded," Inez said, out of breath.

The color drained out of Samuels's face. "You're joking?"

"I'm not. Invaded, infected, boarded. I don't know. Cal doesn't know. Xu and the Doc are trying to figure it out."

"Where's Paul?"

"In the spindle."

"Where's Cal?"

"In the lab with Xu and the Doc, I think."

"What are we supposed to do?"

"Seal the CM." Inez slid the hatch away from the CM's curving wall, and it pivoted into place.

"Because we're being invaded."

"Yes."

"What's happening to the other ship?"

"What? I don't know."

Samuels pivoted and bolted back into her seat. She called up an external camera view. The former moonlet's surface was still quiet. It had hardly moved, continuing on in their shared Jupiter rendezvous orbit. It had just drifted to the rear about three hundred feet beneath the ship. It was turning slowly as if on a spit.

Inez floated up next to her. "Is it dead?"

The pilot reached out and swiped her gloved thumb and forefinger across the screen. The image zoomed in. On closer inspection, they could see there was something occurring. The outer surface was coming apart as a leaf might decay, skin slowly disintegrating to leave empty skeletal cells and warrens behind.

"It looks like it's dying to me."

"It could just be shedding its skin?"

"What, like a snake?"

"Maybe?"

"You're just making this worse."

Twenty-Two

The Doctor placed the sample container on a light panel. Cal bumped his nose against his own faceplate jostling with Xu to get a look at its contents. It was a spattering of silver ash.

The Doc prodded it with a probe. "When I pried this off the wall, it was as resilient as any vine and growing at an observable rate. The second I cut through the tendril, it just fell apart, and the dark red coloration faded away." She replaced the cover of the transparent container and placed the sample into the microscope scanner. A section of the wall illuminated with a large image of the ash. She increased the magnification.

"Look at this, it has a fractal structure. Like a Julia or Mandelbrot set, although there's no true three-dimensional analogue of those number sets in real life, not without extending into other dimensions."

"Does not the structure of much of organic life follow self-similar fractal patterns? Flowers and such?" Zuoren asked.

"It does. And non-organic forms like mountains and coastlines, too, but nothing in nature is infinite. The fractals in nature only repeat for a few levels of magnification. So far, this substance seems mathematically infinite."

"Interesting."

"You can say that again. And it's dissolving. Melting away."

"Into what?"

"Nothing. Finer and finer grains of dust. Losing all complexity, starting from the edges. See here." She panned and zoomed the view.

"Most interesting," Zuoren said.

"Right? This might be a cross-section of a higher dimensional structure." She dialed up the magnification further. "Finer and finer recursive detail at increasing magnifications. Self-similarity straight down to the scope's maximum resolution."

"Which is?"

"Point-five nanometers."

"That's a good microscope."

"I agree, we got our money's worth with that microscope," Xu said.

Cal turned to look at his science officer and smiled at the hapless attempt at a joke from the normally humorless Xu Zuoren.

He turned back to the screen. "So, what does this all mean?"

"It is either a technology or life process that, like fractal imagery, produces complex structures from the application of simple rules."

"And can we define those rules?"

"We should be able to, but it will take some careful measurement and calculation to try and isolate an algorithm that accounts for the structures we're seeing."

"Will that help us either communicate with or combat it?"

"I don't know."

"The rate that thing was growing we may not have the time."

"I concur."

"The tendrils immediately collapsed when cut . . ." the Doctor said as if thinking out loud. "Maybe we don't need to know how it was made, maybe it's enough just to know that we can affect it."

"A fine point, Doctor. The immediate collapse implies that its growth is supported or directed in some way, either from a connected node or a central source point."

"Meaning the fluid bulk and not the moonlet."

"Most likely."

"Is there nothing else you can tell me from this sample?" Cal asked.

Xu looked at the Doctor. "We need to examine the tendrils while they still have animation. There is nothing more we can infer about the active substance from its inactive ash. It's the difference between looking at a fossil and a living specimen."

"We should be able to learn a lot more that way," the Doctor agreed.

Cal looked uncomfortable at the prospect of sending anyone back in there.

"Don't think I didn't analyze a sample of the air in there. I don't believe there are any airborne contaminants," added the Doc.

Cal frowned and opened the comm's tab on his suit's arm screen. "Paul, how are you doing way down there?"

Arthor's face appeared in his HUD. "It's nice here, Cal. Spacious. What have you found out?"

"Not much. It's made of fractals or with fractals. If that rings any bells with you, let me know, but I'm afraid we are going to need to just start taking some stabs in the dark here. Start experimenting. What can we do remotely to affect the docking ring? We need to see what we can do to stop or slow this thing down."

"Evacuate the atmosphere?"

"I don't see where that would have an effect. The vestibule was exposed to vacuum, and the thing obviously was able to handle it."

"True."

"We could increase the atmospheric pressure but, again, it handled the change in pressure when it penetrated the airlock."

"Yeah."

"And I'd be a little worried about over-pressurizing effects on a ship with a compromised airlock."

"What if we draw down the electromagnetic field? Assuming the asteroid moon-object is this thing's ship, it must perform similar functions for it that the *Ulysses* performs for us. If one of those functions is protection, the radiation streaming from the Jupiter-Io flux could be enough to—"

"That's not going to be an option, Cal. We don't even know that it would be affected by the flux, but we certainly will be. Without our protective field, the radiation would kill us almost immediately, and roast the ship's electronics."

"What if we stayed in our suits?"

"They won't help against that much radiation. The only reason you were able to survive a walk outside was because you were still within the *Ulysses*'s electromagnetic field."

"We have to do *something*. We can't just sit here and wait. Can we concentrate the field somehow? Strengthen it within the ring, or the EVA airlock itself, if possible?"

"I'm not sure. It would take a lot of work to reorient the main unit's focus, and we'd have to turn it off, leaving the ship unprotected. I'm sure Xu and I could possibly construct something, but it would take time. A lot of time. And like you said, all for a shot in the dark."

"What about the lander?" asked the Doc.

"The lander?"

"Well, it protects its crew when away from the ship. What if we removed the EM field unit from the lander and set that up at the airlock? Gotta be faster than starting from scratch."

"When we can take these helmets off, I'll kiss you, Doc."

"I'm never taking this helmet off, Cal."

Cal smiled and stepped back to talk to the ship. "Odysseus, you can bring the lander back, can't you?"

"Yes, Captain. The lander is undamaged and still under my control."

"Paul, Xu, and the Doc need a better look at our guest. We're reentering the docking ring."

Twenty-Three

Cal, Xu, and the Doc floated down the central spinal corridor of the ship toward the ring, staring at the interior camera feed as they went. Little seemed to have changed in the forty or fifty minutes since they had evacuated.

"This doesn't make any sense given the growth we had witnessed earlier."

"Could something in the ring be stopping it? Something about our air? Temperature? Pressure?"

"Maybe it stopped of its own accord?"

Cal hesitated at the closed hatch, carrying the silver briefcase. He opened the hatch and drifted into the circular chamber. Blue, red, and green, the three suited figures drifted out and into the space. Gripping onto various handrails, they oriented themselves around the EVA airlock.

"Nothing's changed."

Cal floated closer to the tendrils extending from the border of the lock. "It's changed. They're thicker."

"They've grown too, but only as far as the joint between the wall cladding and the ceiling," Xu said.

"Doc, make your observations. Xu, get that other piece of wall cladding off. We need to see where it's going."

The scientist pulled himself along the curving wall to the equipment locker while the Doc settled, upside-down, on the ceiling like a scuba diver settling onto the sea floor. She removed a set of instruments from her bag. Her field microscope activated as she released it; tiny ducted turbofans held its multiple cameras motionless above the distended red branch bulging through the airlock seal. The magnification appeared on her forearm suit-screen.

Xu returned to the wall with a security torx and began removing the panel adjacent to the one the tendrils had branched across.

The hatch to the spindle opened, and Paul Arthor swam into the room in his orange spacesuit and headed directly for the lander ports. Cal glanced his way and held his hand up, palm out. The big engineer nodded his head in his helmet. He didn't mind waiting, as he hoped Cal would change his mind about extracting the smaller ship's EM field generator and coils. He'd need to remove the module's inner rear wall and some minor plumbing, and come at it backwards given that the EVA airlock was out of commission. It was a lot of work for a plan he disagreed with, but he would carry out the job if asked.

Xu removed the wall panel, revealing a shower of red-black roots that dove into the layer beneath; a domain of tracks of pipes, wiring, and conduits that ran throughout the length of the ship.

"And we thought it hadn't been busy."

"Dear Lord, look at that mess."

"Getting religion, Cal?"

"What are we looking at?"

"It is spreading in dendritic fashion into the innards of the ship. It's bewildering to look at . . . but if we just focus on a single trunk, we can begin to discern some behavior."

Xu used the end of his screwdriver to gesture at the root-like branching. "We can see that it grows outwards along any surface. When it encounters a new object, be it a structural element, conduit, wire, pipe, or wall plate, it sinks a tendril, penetrating the object. What occurs below the surface we will not know until we open up some of these conduits or section a minor support."

"We'll leave the supports alone for now. It's into the RCS thruster feed lines?"

"Yes, Cal."

"O2 and water?"

"Yeah. Potable, probably the cooling water as well. The pipes run all over the ship, it's part of our shielding. Water is an excellent armor against radiation."

"It's in the data lines, too?"

"And electrical, yes."

"Shut down power to the data lines and open them up. I think they're the least essential system in this circumstance. Let's see how deep this goes."

"Roger, Cal," said Paul.

"Take note of a few other behaviors." Xu turned his wrist lights on and gestured deep between layers of conduit and wire to illuminate the ship's outermost insulation layer. "First, it is not growing toward the insulation layer. I don't know if that is because of an aversion to the material or if it is possibly aware of the ship's layout and does not want to penetrate the outer hull."

He gestured along the nearest conduit. "The second thing is the pattern of growth. You can see that the branches nearer to the airlock are larger, reminiscent of the growth of tree limbs. But notice this difference . . ." He waved the tip of his screwdriver. "When a tendril first penetrates a conduit or cable, or whatever, that tendril will grow in diameter, but look at the other tendrils along the same conduit." He moved the screwdriver along the conduit. "The growth pattern shoots roots into the conduit every meter or so, but these tendrils have not enlarged."

"And what does that mean?"

"I do not know. It could suggest planning, cognition, but it could also be mindless plant-like activity. If I had to guess, I'd say that, if we were to open it up, we would find that the first root has tapped the conduit and the others were just looking for an untapped vein, if you'll excuse the potentially unfortunate metaphor."

"Or a potentially accurate one. Open it up."

"Yes, S—"

"What the—"

"Doc?"

"I wanted to get a look at the active interior so I cut into the trunk, and it won't cut. Well, it will cut, but it won't stay cut."

Cal pushed over to where the Doctor had set up her instruments. She was holding a scalpel over a bulging section of root illuminated by the hovering medical drone.

"Watch," she said and sliced into the root. Just as with the column-like arm that the moon-object had extruded, the seemingly solid root broke apart into baroque fragments that flowed as a gel or liquid and shattered into smaller and smaller elements along the same geometry. A shower of ash spiraled away from her scalpel, but beyond the blade, the root's elements flowed back together until it was whole again.

"Xu, cut one of those smaller roots."

The science officer dug into a centimeter-wide root with the bifurcated end of his screwdriver—it plunged right through. The darkly reflective branch flowed around the head of the tool. He selected a smaller bifurcation closer to the leading edge of growth, a tendril about a millimeter in diameter, and again stabbed with his screwdriver. The tendril exploded into a filigree of fine roots that continued their growth.

"How do we stop this thing?" the Doc asked.

"Wait a minute," the engineer said. He pulled his tool bag around from his back, unzipped it, and extracted a roll of duct tape. "How about we treat it not as an infection or infiltration but as a leak?" Paul asked. "It acts like a fluid, maybe we just need to patch the hole where the water's coming in?"

"Go for it."

The big engineer shifted his orientation and floated at a diagonal to the airlock wall and stretched a length of tape out between his gloved hands and lowered the taut strip onto the root as if he were interrupting a flow of water. The tape sunk about an inch into the mass of the root and then slowed as if the water had turned to maple syrup. Paul twisted his features as the tape ceased to cleave into the root and twisted down upon itself. He pulled a tool from the open bag and tapped the surface of the root just beyond the line of tape. He thought he detected some ripples beneath but the fluid had formed a solid surface. He slapped it with the haft of the tool and it bounced out of his grip. Rock-solid.

Cal turned to Xu, who was wielding a scalpel of his own, slicing open the covering of the data conduit like he was dissecting an eel. The insulating layers peeled open one after another at the touch of the blade. A network of fine red-black roots had formed, running inside the conduit, penetrating the wires inside. Here and there, a tendril bulged and luminous sparks of red, green, and blue could be seen moving in the wine-dark depth of the mass, like bubbles, rising toward the surface only to vanish.

"How the hell do we stop this thing?"

"I am haunted by what control said about algorithmic communications."

"How so, Xu?"

"There was mention of the unintended consequences that could result from describing a self-propagating virtual machine to another species. That it could be interpreted as an act of aggression."

"Are you saying we need to be careful of assuming that these acts that seem like infiltration and infection might be attempts at communication?"

"It's possible."

"Xu," the Doc said. "An infection is just communication that kills."

Cal looked at the three of them. "I want you to rip open everything behind this wall, short of the hull, and find out where it's spreading and how fast. See if it's spreading faster in, say, the O2 lines than in the data channel, or whatever. Don't even think about stopping it, just learn more about it."

Twenty-Four

The object, the former asteroidal moon, was beginning to break apart into two roughly equal parts. Samuels had the image up on the large screen in between the two cockpit windows. The last of the moonlet's skin had sloughed away, and the object had been reduced to two sleek recurving masses held together only by the fracturing skeleton of the old structure. Shining dust was blooming into the void as spars and ribs buckled and collapsed.

Inez floated into the nose and pivoted to face Samuels in the left-hand seat. "What's it doing?"

"Mitosis in asteroids? I don't know." She swept her gloved fingers over the console, zooming out of the images. "Still no response?"

"Nothing," Inez said. "Xu is right, it might not be possible for us to understand them. There are ancient languages that remain a mystery, and those were created by humans."

"That's what Xu was saying."

"Have you ever read Lem?"

"No, what's Lem?"

"Lem's a writer. A philosopher. He took the position that without common biological and cultural reference points, there is no possibility of translation, of understanding."

"Common reference points?"

"Yes, core aspects of existence—we all are born and then die, we need food to eat, we reproduce by the combination of two sex cells, we are born under earth's gravity, and mark time as the passing of day and night. Communication without those shared points of reference might be impossible."

"Comforting thought."

The two fell quiet and turned their attention back to the ventral camera feeds. The two shapes were about three hundred feet long, longer than the ship's automated refueling tanks, and many times their girth. The trailing ends of the masses curved to a straight line while the forward ends developed a slight globular aspect. The frail remnants of the moonlet's skeleton shattered into clots and swirls of silvery dust. Disintegrating first to starboard with the port skeleton falling away quickly thereafter. The debris added to the orbiting material swathing the gigantic new shapes in twin banks of glittering clouds.

The pilot tabbed open her comms. "Cal, I have an update."

Twenty-Five

Cal looked up from the image of the bifurcating moonlet on his suit-screen and back at the curving, disassembled wall and the rainbow colors of his crew's spacesuits. They pulled and stacked wall panels and floated around the opening, arrayed in all directions like a flower whose petals were each a different color.

He tabbed open his comms again. "Inez, make sure you get another situation report off to control."

"Will do, Cal."

He pushed off and floated up toward his compatriots around the opening into the arterial maze of pipes and wiring. The blue petal rejoined the flower.

"What's going on out there?" The Doc knew he'd been talking to the CM.

"Crazy shit."

"Crazier than *this?*" She spread a series of windows out onto both of their suit-screens. The images appeared to be of a tendril, focusing on slightly different angles and ever-increasing depths and magnifications. "Full disclosure, I'm going to just start making words up to try and communicate what I'm seeing here because I can't come up with ones to get my point across."

"I understand, Doc. The term is *coining*. You're coining new terms." They smiled at one another.

"The tendrils are a fluidic solid organized, as we saw, along fractal lines. If you take a look at these images here, though, you can see that there are distinct currents within the fractal fluid—some interweaving but not interrupting, other currents flowing in entirely different directions."

"That's fairly amazing, yes?"

"Yes, it is." The Doc enlarged another set of images. "Take a look, this is a representation of voltage change over time, just like an EKG, superimposed over those last images. You can see that there is a modulated electromagnetic flow within all those sub currents. No doubt that's a transmission of information. Whether it is the kind of information a plant gets sent by its roots, or a dog's brain from its paw, or from computer to device, I don't know."

"How'd you collect the voltage changes from the deeper currents without disrupting the structure?"

"I used magnetically-lensed electrodes, why?"

"Any chance that could be responsible for these apparent modulations?"

"I don't think so, Cal. If that were so, I'd think I'd see the same modulations in each area probed. I don't. But in this circumstance, who knows?" She shrugged in her forest green suit.

He turned to his engineer. "They're into everything, Cal. Everywhere. We're going to need to start moving into other sections of the ship to keep following it, but we've taken the cladding all the way off from the airlock port to the main corridor hatch, and they're all through the systems."

"Even the fuel and oxidizer lines?"

"Yeah," Paul replied. "I shut the valves, bled the lines, we opened up the RCS supply and they were in there. Just like everywhere else—little fingers of them with a bigger, arterial-kinda root."

"All these penetrations and no leaks? No pressure changes, no electrical shorts?"

"Nothing. Nothing on the virtual or actual gauges, and I physically tested the penetration points around the O2 lines using the ol' water bubble trick, and I can't find any leaks."

"I've noticed some additional interesting behaviors," Xu said.

"Yes?"

"For some reason, the tendrils are not growing back out beyond the wall cladding."

"Wants to keep out of sight maybe?"

"Or there's something in the atmosphere that's impeding its growth?"

"Maybe."

"What else?"

"I noticed something similar regarding its behavior toward the wiring in our data conduits. If you follow the conduit that we first sliced open, the infiltration actually *leaves* the wiring right at this point here." Xu used his screwdriver to trace the conduit across two wall segments and through apertures in their supporting structural elements to a shielded metal box that connected to a number of other conduits. An inch before the conduit joined with the box, it bristled with a collar of red tendrils that reached around and over the silver RF shield to meet, in grasping fashion, with similar tendrils sprouting from other converging data lines.

"That box is one of Odysseus's processing nodes?"

"Correct."

"The weed is growing out of the conduits before it gets to the node. Leaving them?"

"Yes," Xu replied, reaching in with a gloved hand. The delicate red branches broke and reformed as he spread open a pre-sliced area of conduit insulation. Beyond a certain point, the glowing fibers were completely free of the red weed.

"Something in the nodes is repelling the tendrils?"

"Possibly. Or something about the tendrils is telling them to avoid the processing nodes—and maybe our living spaces."

"Or *someone*."

"Maybe."

"And why?"

"Unknown."

"Maybe the radio frequency emissions that the RF shield is designed to reduce are repulsing the tendrils?"

"We removed the RF shield here, but there was no change. Perhaps if the RF shield were removed before the tendrils matured?"

"The radio frequency emissions might be enough to stop the small tendrils, and if that's true, we could at least halt its spread."

"The main engine uses powerful radio frequency generators to convert hydrogen into plasma. If radio waves leaking from computer chips affect them, I bet we could modify the engine to drive them right out of the ship."

"Where's the nearest unaffected node?"

"There isn't one in the storage ring, so either the one in the centrifuge hub or the one at the top of the spindle that services the cradle. Best guess, the growth shouldn't have spread to either as of yet."

"The one in the cradle is closer. We can remove the RF shield and see what effect that has on the growth of the tendrils. It's our only lead so far. Doc, you're with me."

Cal and the Doc's blue and green suits headed down to the spindle hatch opposite the main corridor.

"Xu, Paul, you keep trying to determine the extent and rate of spread."

"Yes, Cal."

"And leave the wall panels open."

80

Twenty-Six

The Doc followed Cal's blue suited shape as he dropped down the narrow corridor that fell through the carousel and terminated at the engineering hatch in the distance. Unlike the ergonomically pleasing interior forward of the docking ring, with its wall cladding and padded corners, the corridor down through the fuel and consumables system was simply a cramped cylindrical void through the core of a three-hundred-foot-long maze of pipes, wiring, armatures, and soaring trusses. One third down its length, the shaft widened to accommodate a platform with a grated floor and sets of tethers. An emergency suit locker and charging station were set into the curved wall.

Cal dropped to the platform floor next to the suit locker and hopped aside to make the Doc's landing easier. He steadied her with a hand at her shoulder and then tugged at her backpack.

He pointed at the recharge station and pulled a hose out from the wall. She turned around so he could latch it to her backpack's recharging port and then did the same for him. The indicators in her HUD registered the refilling of her oxygen supply and the recharging of her suit batteries.

"We've been in these things awhile, best to top-off before we go outside."

"That's true." The Doc pointed at the maze of pipes above them.

"And before that stuff gets here." Beginning somewhere about twelve to fifteen feet above them and stretching into the heights of the corridor, the piping was taking on a red cast.

Cal tabbed open comms on his forearm screen. "Xu, I don't like what I'm seeing here. This is a *lot* of growth. What concerns me is—where is the mass for that growth coming from? Is it leeching matter from *Ulysses*?"

"If it isn't, and it is additional mass, then we must consider how that will affect the ship's performance and fuel consumption."

"First things first, Xu. We've been quarantined from this stuff in our suits, but we are going to have to get out of them eventually. To delay that inevitability, I want everyone to go to the suit recharging station furthest from the docking ring, there's one in the CM, and start topping off your tanks in case the chargers are infiltrated by the weed."

"Roger, Cal."

"Nutrient fluids too, we don't know the next time we'll have the chance."

"Roger."

"The Doc and I are headed outside to the node. Cal out." He tapped off comms.

"Ready?"

"Ready," replied the Doc.

They opened the inner airlock door, it was identical to the one in the docking ring, and stepped into the vestibule, locking it behind them. A yank downwards on the handle between the two doors and the lights started flashing, red and green swapping sides, and the atmospheric pressure bled from the chamber. Their suits ballooned out slightly. The outer airlock door opened. Beyond Cal's shoulder, all she could see was stars.

Twenty-Seven

Xu stared into the airlock vestibule. The fluid mass had just shattered, the shards still floating in rough approximation of the globule's former shape. The stumps of branches that had penetrated the door stuck out into the space of the airlock; remnants of the mass's former bulk spun around their splintered ends. The globule's mass must have been exuded through the tentacles and dispersed into the ship.

"Paul," Xu spoke into his comms mic. "What's happening there?"

Paul Arthor was in the large circular corridor leading up the spine from docking into the storage ring. Three large cabinets had been removed from the wall and floated nearby. He was pulling insulation back from behind the wall to reveal the conduit layer. An engineering drone hovered nearby, keeping a spotlight on the area where the big engineer was working.

"Same thing, I had to pull one more locker off the wall, but the growth is slowing down in this direction. It's almost stopped."

Xu contemplated. If the red vine had spread in an even fashion from the EVA airlock and ran out of gas here . . . It might not grow as far as Cal's computing node at all. An answer as to whether or not it was the radio frequencies emitted by the electronics that interfered with the growth might not be forthcoming. It was plain to him, however, what was slowing the overall growth. He stared at the empty and broken shell in the airlock. The tendrils had used up the resources they had brought with them, and they were not, at least yet, disassembling the ship in order to continue their growth.

Twenty-Eight

The Doctor reached out and let her fingers brush along the gleaming white flank of a rocket tanker. One of four that the man in the blue spacesuit had so recently, and impossibly, stolen from out of the middle of the first interplanetary revolt. She was gliding down its length, tether at its limit, connecting her to the huge revolving carousel and massive berthing clamps they called "the cradle." Named for the way the clamps cradled the ship's two hundred and fifty-foot-long reusable rockets/fuel tanks. The carousel assembly, engineering, and main engine bell made up half the length of the *Ulysses*, and the cradle comprised fully two-thirds the length of that half.

The stars wheeled beyond the horizon of their ship. Leaving the cramped confines of the spindle and exiting into space, the Doc's senses expanded in all directions around her. A spacewalk was an overwhelmingly humbling and awesome experience. A person risked losing herself in it, losing her mind possibly, but the sight of the ship was her anchor. The *Ulysses* and the menacing shapes revolving just diagonally off her flanks. Or was it off her dorsal and ventral sides? With a vessel like *Ulysses*, it was hard to tell.

Cal had ceased his motion by applying the brake on his tether and expertly brought himself to a bouncing stop against the exterior of the cradle, near the first set of colossal robotic clamps that secured the tanker. The Doc followed, bounding a little less expertly to a stop. Cal was already opening the panel at the base of the clamps, nestled in a cleft between two runs of insulated cable.

He removed the outer panel, pinched off the valves of the cooling matrix, and secured the panel to an adjacent hull plate with a magnet so it wouldn't drift off. Under the ship's skin there were two layers of insulation blanket plus one gel layer to carefully peel away in order to get at the node, one of Odysseus's autonomic distributed servers. The Doc turned on her glove lights and aimed them over Cal's shoulder and in and around the internal space.

"I don't see it anywhere, do you?"

"No," Cal said. It hadn't spread this far yet. "I'll get this cover off."

He pulled a screwdriver from his belt and removed the safety cap. The plastic impregnated tip prevented the metal of the screwdriver from cold-welding, fusing with the metal of the screws. He took care to pluck each magnetic screw from the tip of the tool and deposit it in a plastic bag glued to the node's case for just such purpose. The RF shield floated free, and he thought for a moment about flinging it off into space but he refrained, attaching it to the magnetic stripe on the back of his pack.

He and the Doc spent the next few minutes wrangling the layered elements back into place, unsealing pinch-valves and replacing the outer skin panel.

They decided to leave the panel loose for ease of access when they returned to check on the weed growth and just wrangled the layered elements into position. He replaced the outer panel using just two screws.

"We're headed back in. Any thought to how long we wait to check and see if that impeded the weed growth in any way?"

"I'm sorry Cal, we've just made a discovery that may make your experiment superfluous."

"Xu, vocab words."

"Sorry, Cal, weed growth seems to have slowed almost to a stop.

We think it's running out of raw materials to create new structure."

This was ostensibly good news, but once again, he felt foiled, two steps behind what might not even be a sentient opponent. Every time he felt like he was closing in on being able to penetrate some mystery of its behavior, it confounded him with change. It had been a grueling day-long race, and he had been bested at every turn.

"Got it," was all he said.

"The growth could still reach you, so your experiment might not be a total loss."

While Cal talked with Xu, he stared out into the gulf with a grimace on his face. The Doc nestled her back against the spindle, between the bulk of two tankers and followed his gaze across space to the alien shape to port.

Solidified into a tapering cylinder with a bulbous front end, the half-moonlet had completed its migration to their flank. The sparkling clouds of debris surrounding it seemed to be coalescing, or being drawn up into, a step-pyramid that was erupting from the cylinder's underside. From the tip and four corners of each of the pyramid's steps, gossamer strands emerged. The filaments seemed wispy and tenuous at this distance, but both of them knew that those pyramids had to be twenty or thirty feet across and those wispy strands were probably the width of one of their thighs. They were growing toward the ship.

The pilot's face bloomed open on Cal's suit-screen, and shouted, "Cal!"

"I see it, Sarah. Put some distance between us and them. I don't like the look of those things."

"Roger, Cal."

"Just a short burst from the main engine, I don't want to warp our Jupiter approach much if we can help it. Give us a few minutes to clear the area. I'll ping you when we're back in the spindle."

"No can do, Cal. Thrusters are fine, but you two can't be anywhere south of the docking ring when we fire the main."

"All right, I won't argue. I suppose they're not growing that quickly. I'll ping you when we're back in the ring. Just be ready to go."

"Right, I'm doing the calculations now."

Cal paid attention to his breathing as they skimmed along the outer spindle, taking the time to wonder why moments of vast beauty like this always reminded people that they were so very small. That their lives were so fleeting.

The rocket tankers in the clamps to either side of them blotted out the stars. Over and ahead, the absolute black, the Milky Way seemingly washed from existence due to the glare of the spotlights illuminating the shapes of the cradle. The alien object was hidden from view.

Cal felt his thoughts of impermanence were inappropriate. The key to being able to live life, day to day, was the ability to deny the very mortality that defines us. To envision life as unlimited and to act as if it would continue forever. It was self-delusion, a shade of madness and without it, he figured, all of humanity would go insane.

Cal and the Doc reentered the airlock. It was overgrown with the red weed.

"I thought Xu said it had stopped?" the Doc asked, turning around to stare at the red tinted maze of conduits and pipes.

"He did, it must have stopped growing there but not here." Cal shifted his feet on the metal grating and peered "down" the spindle, toward the engineering ring. "It looks like its spread pretty far down. I think it might have already reached the node."

"Are we going back out?"

"Obviously, the weed is growing in some places, retreating in others, using its mass where it needs it. It's not so much growing as *creeping.*"

"Are we going back *out?*"

"I am."

"Then I am, too." The Doc reached past Cal and swung the lever to reopen the inner airlock door.

88

Twenty-Nine

Two brightly-suited forms stood along the long axis of the carousel and gazed down toward the engine bell. They stepped out onto the curved surface, tankers and clamps rising around and away to either side. The stars shone like broken glass scattered across blacktop. The port side *thing* hung menacingly against this backdrop. Cal turned his blue-helmeted head to the Doc and said, "I can do this a lot quicker if you'll just stay here, Susan."

She was half-relieved, half consumed with indignant fire. She looked down at the cradles again and then out at the alien object and the self-assembling framework that was extending toward the *Ulysses* with alarming speed. This wasn't about bravery or playing her part, it was about what was needed in the moment. She nodded.

Cal smiled, disengaged his magnets and threw himself down through the carousel. Skimming the surface of the spindle, he sailed along between two of the tankers. Approaching the first set of clamps, Cal drew his legs up into his stomach and somersaulted end over end to reposition his body with his legs perpendicular to the surface. He re-magnetized his boots and brought his feet down close to the ship's skin. The pull began to exert a slight drag, and then he stopped with a jolt as the soles of his boots made full contact with the spindle. Sharp pain shot through his left knee, reminding him that he'd probably sprained it that morning—the first time that day he'd used the electromagnets in his boots so creatively.

The pain wrapped around his knee and burned down his shin, but he grimaced and ignored it. He grabbed a tool from his belt and removed the fasteners that held the panel against the framework beneath. The panel drifted free as he pulled aside the layers of insulation and cooling mesh. Gouts of ash billowed out, distal tendrils of red weed breaking apart as the layers paged open. In the brief time they had been inside, the weed had reached the node. Tendrilous growth burst from the conduits leading to the server and skirted around it. Exactly the same as before. The RF emissions made no difference. The weed was avoiding the node for some other reason. He balled his fists in frustration, resisting the urge to punch the hull, because of Newton's third law, and then set about a few minutes of hurriedly pushing the layers back into the gap in the hull, releasing pinch-valves, and securing the cover in place. With only one of the four screws.

He pivoted in space, turning parallel to the ship's long axis, and pushed off with his hands to sail up through the cradle.

Thirty

The pilot was ready for the burn, but she stared at the images coming in from the cameras out of the corner of her eye. She took a long draw off the nozzle built into the helmet of her suit. Orange nutrient drink, the classic. She loved it.

The structures growing outwards from the alien cylinders were solidifying as they reached for the ship in a reverse process of the disintegration that she had witnessed previously. Secondary frameworks were growing within the skeleton, an external skin forming between buttresses and spars. Sparks coruscated around the points of the inverted ziggurats at the tips of the booms. New girders and struts exuded from a nimbus of condensing smog.

The shape and arrangement of the two objects were beginning to suggest a great disembodied set of insectile mandibles opening wide, ready to close down on the ship.

They needed to get the hell out of there.

Thirty-One

In the perfect clarity of the vacuum, the Doc watched Cal rise up along the exterior of the spindle to her perch aside the airlock door.

As he reached her level, she helped steady him and arrest his motion.

"What am I missing, Doc?" He was breathing heavily.

She opened the outer airlock door. In green and blue suits, they stepped into the vestibule and she pulled the door shut behind them.

"I don't know, Cal. I'm not sure that you're missing anything at all."

"That's what I'm afraid of."

The lights cycled from red to green. They opened the interior airlock door and stepped back inside the infested spindle. He pushed off from the platform and headed toward the docking ring, anguished by the presence of the twisting, questing growth. The Doc followed. Cal searched for commonalities in the behavior of the vine, trying to divine intent.

"Maybe it's avoiding computational centers? It's avoiding Odysseus's processors and, by staying in the walls, the only other calculating beings around—us."

"The human brain is not a computer," objected the Doc. "But I get your point. Maybe it is avoiding *thinking* beings for some reason?

Altruism? Quarantine?"

"And that's why its staying behind the walls, not invading our living spaces."

"Maybe."

"We *have* to figure out what it wants." Cal pushed against the wall for more speed, careful to avoid anything red. "The thing is going anywhere it *wants* to. It's infiltrated every system. But not the ship's brains—because it doesn't *want* to. Would it infiltrate our bodies if it could, and would it avoid our brains as well?"

"I don't know, but it's a good thing we haven't taken off our helmets yet." The Doc smiled behind the reflections in her faceplate.

Cal hit the hatch at the end/top of the tight corridor. He braced himself against the circular walls, twisted the hatch and threw it open. As soon as the Doc cleared the hatchway, he pinged the command module.

Thirty-Two

Samuels pulled the console to her and gripped the control stick. With her left index finger, she pushed the thrust slider to 80 percent. She held the finger down on the *command* button in order to set a timer for the upcoming burn.

"Thirty seconds to main," she said into the comms. "Feed to mission control open, hope y'all enjoy the show—despite the forty-four-minute delay." She opened a new display window and tapped checks into boxes on the screen.

"Propellant injectors?"

"Check."

"RF generator one?"

"Check.

"Helicon coupler?"

"Check."

"Superconducting magnet array?"

"Check."

"Ion cyclotron heater coupling?"

"Check."

"RF generator two?"

"Check."

"Magnetic confinement nozzle?"

"Check."

"Reactor output?"

"361 megawatts at 71 percent efficiency," replied the ship's AI.

Seventy-one percent. She smiled and tightened her grip on the control stick. Paul Arthor was getting 3 percent more out of *Ulysses*'s reactor than Anise Hamilton had squeezed from the *Eureka's* on their last run.

"Thank you, Odysseus."

"Twenty-five seconds to main engine ignition."

The tolerances of the *Ulysses*'s main engine were so precise and the forces of its operation so great that every functional component was magnetically shielded while running. None of the engine surfaces were in actual physical contact with anything else during normal operations, not even the propellant.

She opened another window on the console's screen and flicked a control tab to maximum.

"EM field to full."

On the monitor screen, mounted at the crest of module two's cockpit windows, the rear view showed her the alien pincers drawing closer to the ship. The terminal ends of each prong were glistening with newly formed trellises. It was obvious to her that those things were closing in on *Ulysses*, trying to capture the ship via furious construction.

"Ten seconds," said the AI.

"Injectors on." She stabbed the corresponding button as soon as it appeared on the display.

At the top of *Ulysses*'s main engine, triply-redundant valves were opening. Hydrogen gas was being pumped under pressure into the core of the engine—a tapering hollow cylinder bored from titanium.

"Nine seconds."

"RF generator one running. Helicon at 98 percent."

The gas began to be bombarded by low frequency radio waves

emitted by antennae wrapped around the engine cylinder. The waves stripped electrons off the surging propellant, producing a plasma of ions and free electrons. The temperature inside the engine rose to nearly ten thousand degrees, just slightly hotter than the surface of the sun.

"Seven seconds."

"Throttling RF for high thrust and low specific impulse exhaust." The pilot swept open a new window and adjusted a luminous dial.

The second radio frequency generator powered up. At the same time, superconducting magnets surrounding the cylinder began to constrict the flow of newly produced plasma, accelerating its passage through the engine.

"Five seconds."

"Ion cyclotron heater running."

A second antenna coil began swamping the engine with more electromagnetic waves, narrowing its EM field, achieving resonance with the orbits of ions and free electrons streaming past. Thus amplified, the temperature of the plasma spiked to over 1.8 million degrees Fahrenheit.

"Three seconds."

"Magnetic confinement nozzle collimated."

"One second."

The countdown timer expired, and her finger on the joystick's deadman's trigger was enough to allow the process to continue.

"Ignition."

The ions and electrons flew on tight linear orbits through the engine and out into an expanding magnetic field, ejecting them at ever-mounting velocities. A luminous cone of blue-flecked white expanded into being inside the *Ulysses*'s engine bell.

And vanished.

Thirty-Three

"What the hell just happened?" Cal reached the CM just as the engine shut down.

"We lost the injectors, they just powered down," said Samuels, frantically tabbing through open status screens.

Cal craned his head, peering through one of the tiny windows at the rear of the large command module. The little window was one of the telltale signs of *Ulysses*'s modular construction, it was too small and the bulk of the ship too large to afford much of a view. The CM was capable of functioning as a short-range re-entry capable spacecraft of its own. The window was meant only for docking. Still, he could see most of the portside object. The expanding pylon growing from it was largely hidden, but he could picture it relentlessly closing in on his ship.

"And the RF generators. Just lost power, they're off."

"What's going on?"

"I don't know, but I'm ejecting the remaining plasma while we still have control of the engine." The pilot pressed a combination of lights that appeared across the console.

"Helicon and cyclotron are down, too."

Cal held up his left forearm and tapped on his suit-screen. "Paul?"

"I'm on it."

He could see from the video that the engineer was at his station in the docking ring. "I'm reading power to all those systems, Cal."

"They're not powered," said the pilot.

"I know they're not powered, but they've got power."

"Huh?"

"Meaning there's nothing wrong with them, they were just switched off."

"I didn't switch off anything. Are you sure your console isn't malfunctioning? Giving false readings?"

"I'm not sure of anything, but isn't it just as likely that this weed is the cause of the engine shutdown? Interrupt any of the engine's components and the whole thing will shut down to prevent it from destroying itself."

"It *is* into the ship's wiring, particularly the data lines. It's not hard to imagine that interrupting the clean transmission of data might cause an engine component to shut down," said Cal.

"This could also be an unrelated problem, a coincidence," said Xu, also still in the docking ring.

Samuels rolled her eyes. "In triple-redundancy systems?"

"Dammit, Xu!" Cal unconsciously moved his forearm screen closer to his faceplate. "I think we've made enough excuses for it, don't you? We have to figure out how to get rid of this thing!"

"Cal, I know this is a difficult situation, but it's also a historic one. I don't want us to blow first contact with alien intelligence!"

"Xu, they're taking over the ship."

"Cal."

"They're taking over the ship, Xu." He could see that his science officer was nervously stroking the material of his spacesuit's arm.

"Maybe not, Cal. Maybe it just *looks* that way to us."

Samuels broke into the channel. "Are you fuckin' kidding me?"

"No, no. I'm not kidding you. Maybe it's . . . learning."

"Xu, it doesn't matter if its intelligent or not when the net effect is still that it's two steps ahead of us at every turn. We've done nothing but react since the encounter began, and now it's deprived us of control over our ship!" Cal turned his attention to the monitor screen and the rear view from the cradle.

The alien shapes floated just a few hundred feet away, flanking the ship on both sides. Their grasping mandibles had grown so close to the ship as to be beyond the current camera's field of view. He switched to the camera on the exterior dorsal side of the docking ring. So close to the hull now, sparkling light coruscated around the tips of trusses and spars as if they were being pulled into existence by an invisible spiraling printhead. They were white-hot from the energy of the activity. The alien objects had nearly completed twin bridges spanning the gulf between each of them and the interplanetary ship.

"They're going to hit the fucking fuel tanks."

Xu jetted over to the docking ring's panoramic windows. "No, no, no."

"Paul, we need the engine. Right away."

"I'm on my way down the spindle now. I'll be in the engineering ring in five . . . but, Cal."

"I know."

"I can eject the tanks."

"What would be the point? Then we'd be dead no matter what."

"At least then we might get to see Jupiter before we die."

"Try to light the engine and if worse comes to worst . . ." Cal paused.

"What?"

"Worse comes to worst, we find out if they're good aliens or bad aliens."

Thirty-Four

Paul Arthor soared down the spindle, kicking off at various practiced points during the descent, red weed or no. He hit the bottom of the corridor and was quickly through the hatch, descending into the module at the very rear of the spaceship. Beyond that lay only the curve of the engine bell and empty space.

The engineering ring circled the reactor complex and the engine itself, providing nearly three-hundred and sixty degrees of access to the hardware over four zero-G levels. Its placement behind the mass of consumables stored in the rocket tankers helped shield the majority of the ship from radiation. Most of the time, Arthor accessed the engineering systems from his control station in the front half of the ship, on the other side of all that shielding mass. Whenever possible, though, he preferred to be in engineering itself rather than using drones. Otherwise, what was the point of having a human aboard? What was the point of *being* human?

First order of business was to confirm what the engineering station in the docking ring was telling him. He sailed over to the side of the module devoted to engine controls. The consoles and flooring on that side were all different shades of blue. Reactor side was red. He moved to a panel on the console at the center of the room, right up next to the engine housing. The panel was transparent and behind it, actual, physical gauges and indicators. They all read identical to what the engineering console was telling him. There was no interference, *Ulysses*'s computers seemed to be functioning properly. He looked around the ring, there was no red weed here either.

He ducked under the console and jammed his screwdriver into all four corners successively in rapid motion, releasing the fasteners. The wall panel dropped away, and he yanked on a conduit inside to pull it out from the housing. He carefully sliced into the insulation with his utility knife; the conduit parted and its gut of fibers and wire were revealed. Normally, half of those were brightly illuminated fibers. In this conduit, they were dark.

No weed but no power.

He floated up to the hatch, opened it, and pulled himself up into the spindle corridor and its maze of conduit and pipe. He located the nearest data conduit and made another incision. No weed, no power.

A forceful push sent him shooting upwards. He closed his hand around a large pipe and slowed his ascent until he was among the tendrils. He stopped by grabbing a data conduit and sliced into it. Red weed puffed into silver flakes as the insulation parted, bright light poured out from illuminated wires.

Paul tapped his fingers on the curve of his forearm screen. "Cal, the weed is definitely interfering with the flow of data to the engines. It's probably interfering with everything beyond a certain point, certainly the electrical system. Where there's red weed, there is power. Where the weed stops, power stops and I don't know why. We're not going to be able to fire the main. Not anytime soon."

Thirty-Five

Cal had moved to the docking ring and watched helplessly as the boiling tips of the alien buttresses contacted his ship. A slow-motion crash into the *Ulysses* just below the docking ring, right above the four rocket tankers filled with liquid hydrogen, oxygen, and water, into an area known as the forward wheel. The wheel girdled the ship, connecting the carousel and cradle to the docking ring. The refueling transport lines, rotational motor and gear, the armatures that mated to the noses of the tankers, and their support equipment were all housed on the forward wheel.

Cal had every status window spread out over the nearest console's display. From the corner of his eye he kept watch for indications of damage to the ship's operations, tank levels, or pressure vessel integrity.

The alien structural elements continued to collapse into the ship. At the point of intersection, additional spars and supports began to inscribe themselves into existence, further reinforcing the weld between the earth ship and the alien.

The wheel was an integral component of the spacecraft—but it was almost strictly a structural element, a mounting platform for instruments and equipment. Like the carousel, it had no habitable spaces, the spindle merely passed through its center.

If you were going to attach something to the *Ulysses*, the wheel was where you'd do it.

Plant-like intelligence, my ass, thought Cal.

He watched as a pearlescent skin began to close over the pylon's framework, hiding its interior. Just before it grew shut, Cal thought he glimpsed other structures forming and trunks of red weed coursing beneath.

"Now what?" he asked himself before realizing that was the wrong question. "What do we do now?" That was more like it.

Thirty-Six

Paul Arthor set searchlight drones orbiting around the ship, illuminating as best he could the twin alien pylons that had sunk deep into one of the main structural elements supporting the carousel and its cradle of rocket tankers. The alien cylinders were joined to the ship, flanking it with perfect symmetry. Floating buttresses, braced against the hull in such a way that they appeared entirely more permanent than had the rapidly extruded boarding tunnel. The tunnel was temporary but had delivered the red weed. What would this new invasion bring?

Add that to the list, he thought, along with, *why did it split in two? And what the fuck does it want?*

He spared a glance at the glow from the exposed data lines. No vermillion had suffused the blue-white pulse of the ship's optical net. The red weed had not yet come for the heart of the ship.

The question foremost on his mind was what was the extent of the damage to the forward wheel, the equipment it housed, and to the structure of the ship itself?

Bafflingly, but par for the course, the answer seemed to be *almost none.* Apart from superficial damage at the collision site, which was rapidly being obscured by newly generated material, there wasn't a ship's system that strayed off nominal for more than the fluttering of an eyelid.

Two huge physical structures had attached to or been embedded in the ship and yet nothing seemed to have been affected by it. As if the ship were designed for it, which it wasn't, of course. The one thing he knew had to be affected was the ship's performance and fuel consumption. The mass of the objects was an unknown that needed to become known.

He looked at the multiple drone viewpoints displayed on his console, examining the shape of the alien objects and their relation to the shape of the ship itself. Somehow, it looked right to him. Complementary. Despite himself, it pleased him aesthetically.

His comms channel beeped; he raised his left forearm. Cal's blue helmeted face appeared on the screen.

"Cal, you're looking at this, I assume."

"Yeah, your opinion?"

"First of all, whatever it is, it was designed to attach to the *Ulysses*. It probed us and then redesigned itself to attach to us."

"I would agree. Continue."

"And, if you'll forgive me, it's attached itself in what has ended up to be a very . . . artful manner. There's something elegant about the geometry of it."

"Yes. Symmetry. What do you think they are?"

"To me, they look like engines. But then again, they would, wouldn't they? They could be just about anything else."

"Thanks, Paul." Cal cut his feed.

The engineer returned his attention to the drone video.

Have to be engines, he thought. *What else could they be?*

Thirty-Seven

"They're crew pods," the pilot said.

"What?" asked Inez, strapped into her communications seat in the CM's rear.

"They're inside them, more of those blob things."

"That doesn't make any sense, if there were more, why wouldn't they have come over when that first blob did?"

"Maybe that first one was a scout, and now that they've seen that we can't stop them . . ."

"Maybe but it doesn't make sense to me, but then again nothing has made sense to me so far, so maybe they are crew pods." She tapped a yellow gloved finger against her station. Waveforms of meaningless static reeled continuously across the screens.

"Why do you think it's grabbed us?"

"I'm not going to speculate; we're going to find out."

"I guess so but I can't help it." Samuels turned her gaze to the gas planet, shining with incredible clarity and dominating the view from the cockpit windows despite the vast space between.

Thirty-Eight

Cal spun away from the lower sweep of windows and crossed the ring to float alongside Xu. "What do you think they are? Engines?"

"I don't think I can speculate. I'm not sure if my instincts are correct lately."

"Your instincts are fine, Xu. I need and respect your viewpoint. Someone has to play devil's advocate. I always want to hear it, even if I ignore it." He smiled.

"No, I have to apologize. I lost my composure. I was sure that this was a strange but innocuous encounter. I didn't want to believe first contact could be a negative one, but I may have allowed my hopes to override my better judgement."

"Believe me, I hope you're right."

"And I hope you're wrong."

"Odds are good, I've been wrong all day."

"I can't think of anything I'd have done differently in your place."

"Thanks." Cal arched his back and stretched in his suit, the motion making him rotate in place. "I feel like I've been in this thing forever."

"I'm sure we all feel that way."

"The Doctor feels that we should stay in our suits, isolated from the weed as much as possible, for as long as is possible."

"I don't disagree with her."

"Me neither, it's just starting to reek in here."

"I'm ripe."

Cal smiled. "Where is the Doc?"

"The zero-G lab." Xu turned back to the open wall sections and refocused the field microscope he'd temporarily mounted to the airframe.

Cal sailed up through the hatch and into the corridor, moving through the storage ring, the centrifuge hub, and then into the lab. The lab comprised one half of the sciences ring, the workspace module directly aft of the CM. The Doc's sick bay lab was focused on human biology and keeping people alive and healthy in space. During a mission, sick bay was usually under gravity and was designed with that in mind, so it made sense that she was in the zero-G lab instead. The shared laboratory was outfitted to investigate the atmosphere of Jupiter and samples collected from its choice moons and was much more of a general science lab.

The Doc was in a station chair straining against her seat harness. She had removed the wall panel and rotated the microscope cameras around so that she could observe an active weed with an optical instrument.

"Anything interesting?"

"Everything. Useful? I don't know. The cylinders outside, they've attached themselves to us?"

"Yes."

"More tendrils?"

"I don't know yet. I thought I observed some inside the cylinders as they made their connection, but I'm not sure. Haven't had time to go over the video. Mercifully, the growth of the weed inside the ship seems to have slowed, although who knows how long that will last. Paul and Xu and I have been trying to assess the damage from the collision."

"And?"

"The ship seems fine, although I am finding it hard to believe. We've gotten drones in very close. Close enough for detailed examination of the forward ring structure and, except for the punctures to port and starboard, there are hardly even hairline cracks. As for the punctures, those are being sealed by the growth of the . . . whatever they are. We need to start coming up with agreed upon names for these things.

"We do; I vote for *Thingies*."

Cal smiled weakly. "The ring is entirely a supportive structure, no interior volumes. Any infiltration of equipment mounted around or to the rim should be visible from the outside, so Xu is keeping watch."

"What's got you thinking?" She knew him and knew he was there to talk something out. Cal never came to her about his health, he came to her because they had a lot in common, but she thought very differently than he did. She always had.

"The way it crashed into us," he answered. "That was as gentle an impact as I've ever seen. More like it connected with us . . . It reminds me of the way it deflected the lander during its original approach. Gentle force."

"What does any of this mean?"

"I'm not sure. Maybe it means that despite what seems like aggressive behavior, there is some measure of . . . respect for us in a way?"

"How do you mean?"

"I'm not sure I know myself, but despite my fears, this didn't seem like the pursuit of a predator. Great care was taken to minimize damage during a process where, nonetheless, damage was inflicted."

"It doesn't make sense."

"No, it doesn't, does it?"

"It wants to connect with us, not kill us."

"That's my gut."

"So, Xu's right, this is just a scary form of communication?"

"Not necessarily, it could still be bad. Could be that they just want to take us intact."

They looked at each other in silence for a moment. Space helmet to space helmet. Blue to green.

"But that's silly, what would they want with our ship when they can do all *this?*"

"Maybe they like their specimens alive?"

More silence. For the first time in a while, Cal found himself in front of a window that didn't look out on some aspect of alien horror. Instead, the curved window inset in the lab's wall revealed the spectacle of the approaching Jovian planet and its pageant of moons and tenuous rings. He lost himself in it for a few seconds that felt like hazy minutes.

"How's the suit holding up?"

He checked the battery and O2 indicators in his HUD. "Seventy, seventy-eight."

"That's not bad."

Cal slumped and floated backwards, bumping into the wall.

"You must be exhausted, Cal. I know I am."

"I am. I was just saying to Xu that the suit is wearing on me. Pardon the phrase."

"Yeah, but we need to stay inside as long as possible."

"I told him that, too."

"But I can't wait to get out of this thing."

"I have to pee so bad."

"So, pee in the suit."

Cal wrinkled his nose. "It smells bad enough in here as it is." No matter how much technology was applied to that problem, no one liked going to the bathroom in their pants. He looked at the Doc. "Did you pee in your suit?"

"I peed when the tunnel broke up. I thought that thing was going to hit us. That was the first time, the second time I peed was just earlier."

Cal laughed.

"Are we going to die, Cal?"

"Not if I can help it, Susan."

"Can you help it, Cal?"

"I'm not sure."

Thirty-Nine

Cal gathered the entire crew in the centrifuge hub, just forward of the ship's midline. A rainbow array of suit colors floating in the padded zero-G space. Insulated conduits, filled with everything from data lines to drinkable water, were visible behind any surface that could not be covered by wall cladding.

The multicolored figures bobbed in space, displaying a strange calm that Cal decided at least partly stemmed from exhaustion. They had been pumping adrenaline through their systems for hours upon hours. It was mentally and physically taxing—and spending hours on end inside a spacesuit was trying on the best of days.

"Has anyone any further encroachment to report?"

He looked at their faces.

"Nothing, it seems to be staying put. Don't ask me why," Xu said. He was visibly worn.

"All right, the good news is that I think that we can assume it's not going to kill us anytime soon." He paused to look for disagreement. Samuels seemed as if she was going to say something, but she also looked like she was anticipating what he was about to say and didn't want to be the one that spoiled things.

"Then I suggest we extend the habitats and spin up the centrifuge.

I need to get out of this friggin' spacesuit. Besides, it will provide us with areas of living space further away from the growth of the weed, and I can't see how those things out there are collision threats anymore."

"Not when they've attached themselves to our goddamn ship."

"Doc, have you found any further evidence that the weed spreads in ways other than direct growth?"

"No."

"Nothing airborne?"

"Nothing that I or the cabin air sensors have been able to detect."

"All right, then. Although the Doc is recommending we stay in the suits and even though every time I've seen a scary space movie and they take their helmets off I scream *never take your helmet off*, I'm saying you can use your personal discretion. I won't fault anyone that wants a shower. Just be prepared to get in line behind me."

Cal threw a switch, the crew cheered as the 290-foot arms began to accordion out around them. Stretching to either side, the corridor expanded as the habitats drew further and further away.

They cheered again as the locks released. The pressure rose as additional air was pumped in to help inflate the arms. After a good eight minutes the corridors stretched to their ultimate length and began to rotate. The candy colored spacesuits raced down the arms to get in line for one of the only two showers onboard.

Forty

"Woof, that smelled like living in a fart." Cal pulled the blue helmet off his head and stuck it to the magnetic panel at the foot of the sick bay bunk. His quarters were at the furthest end of Red Hab, and directly across from the everyday crew bathroom, but he chose the sick bay shower as it was much larger. He stood; gravity was just under Mars-normal on this level—about one third that of Earth. He glanced across the sick bay before pulling the accordion-style privacy curtain closed. The bunk across the way was occupied by the form of the Doc in her green spacesuit, propped onto her side by the bulk of her life support backpack. One arm thrown across her stomach, the other dangling toward the floor, her chest rose and fell evenly. The Doc was asleep in her suit.

Cal, obviously, was not. He felt horribly vulnerable with an alien construction attached and only partial control of his ship, but he was exhausted, and he was going to sleep in a bed even if it killed him. But not before a shower.

He pulled the zipper, stripped out of his suit, and walked comfortably to the shower, wrapping a towel around his waist. It felt good not to float. He stepped in and zipped the plastic walls to the halfway mark, hung his towel on the outside hook, and zipped the rest of the way up. A turn of the valve and the water fell in a beautiful slow-motion fan around him. He spun the scratched silver band around his ring finger, feeling the water spatter off his face. Nothing was more luxurious on a space mission than gravity for a shower. He reveled in it for the three minutes of allotted water pressure, turned on the reclamation impeller in the drain, unzipped the wall and let the steam out into the room.

He put on his jumpsuit and squeezed back into his spacesuit as he mused on simple pleasures. The feeling of a long dive from the gravity of one habitat, through the weightlessness of the hub and down the other arm, and into the gravity of the opposite hab was one of the secret joys of the ship. Cal loved to unhook the tender on the ladder cable, climb to the edge of a hab's gravity, check everyone's location to make sure he wasn't going to hit anyone, and dive through the arms, feeling the air rush out of his way. With a little practice, he could land gently in the far hab. It was a glorious feeling. Flying peaceful and serene. Cal gathered up his helmet and stowed it under his arm and jumped. He was in need of some serene.

By the time he had reached the weightlessness of the hub, alarms were going off all over the ship.

Forty-One

"Tank pressures in the cradle are rising. All the consumables. Hydrogen and oxygen pressures are both rising but so are water pressures. Cooling water as well as drinkable water." The pilot had reached the CM and was reading off her console display.

"That doesn't make sense. Why would the drinking water levels be rising? There's no possibility of a cross between any of those other systems and potable water. Why are those tank volumes rising? A carousel-wide failure?" Cal opened a channel to his engineer. "Paul, I need to know what's going on."

"I'm looking at the gauges themselves, your read is right."

"Are we sure? Zero-G tank readings can be iffy."

"I'm pretty sure, Cal. The main engine didn't fully fire, but we got enough of a push to serve as an ullage burn and settle the fuel in the tanks. I think those readings are accurate."

"Are we in danger here?"

"If the pressure keeps rising, yeah."

"Can you release the valves and relieve the pressure manually?"

"I should be able to, either from here or outside."

"Still rising," said the pilot.

"Get ready, Paul. Has the weed spread down there?"

"No, it must have gotten into the tanks from the top, through the carousel."

"Or be screwing with computer control over the valves."

"It's in the data lines, not the computers themselves," Xu retorted as he shot into the CM, fully suited. It was obvious he was rattled but the man kept his composure. He quickly activated his science station and brought up a ship's status window.

"It could still be affecting the data the computers are interpreting," Paul countered. "I thought it had stopped growing?" He added after a moment, "Why is this happening now?"

"Maybe the collision?"

"Xu, are you seeing any tendrils growing on the surface of the wheel?"

"I don't see any, Cal, but that doesn't mean they aren't there."

"Pressure holding steady," Samuels intoned.

"And nothing growing from our two new guests?"

"The twins, Cal? No. Nothing that I can see. The wheel is a mostly solid structure, but there are small internal spaces where it could grow. You think the tendrils are going to try and connect to the twins?"

"Of course, I do."

"We know the tendrils, the weed, that originated from the blob has spread most of the way down spindle. It's possible that it's grown through the walls, out into the carousel."

"And into the rocket tankers through the caps?"

"Or through the consumables transfer lines."

"Through the wall without a pressure drop?"

"Who knows?"

"It hasn't grown through the wall anywhere else."

"That doesn't mean anything."

"What's the read now?" Cal could see the values on the screen but asked anyway.

"Holding steady in the red."

"Paul, vent the lines. Release the pressure."

"Roger, Cal."

"Tank pressures dropping now," the pilot reported.

"I didn't do anything," Paul said.

"Dropping in all the tanks?"

"All of them."

"Did it hear us?" Inez asked.

"I'd say coincidence," said Xu.

"I agree," said the engineer.

Cal looked surprised.

"I do, it's coincidence but something's not right. The pressure was holding steady for a bit. If it was going to keep rising, I'd think it would have already."

"That doesn't make sense."

"It does if the weed is infiltrating the consumables systems. We've seen how the first tendril that sinks into a pipe enlarges. I think it's some kind of a taproot. All you need is one to start adding to or subtracting from a system. If it's tapping into all of these systems and experimenting—"

"That could account for what we are seeing."

"It could."

"Experimenting?"

"There must be a reason behind where it chooses, by thought or instinct, to grow."

"The reason is obvious. It's taking over the ship, or at least giving itself the option."

"For what purpose?"

"That's the question, huh?"

"Still dropping."

"Paul, is there a way we can see inside the tanks?"

"Inside the tanks?"

"We have to get a picture of what it's doing. If it's tapping the tanks, we have to know how."

"There are engineering cameras inside the tankers. I can pull up the feeds," offered Paul.

"Do it." Cal floated back toward the rear of the command capsule to take in the large screen between the windows. It lit up, showing a volume illustrated by concentric rings of circular metallic reflections—the inside of one of the four rocket's largest tanks. It should have been filled with a globular mass of cryogenically cooled liquid hydrogen, sloshing around the shining interior, but it wasn't. Instead, there was something else within the space, a smooth globe of red-black viscosity bouncing in slow motion. The mass occupied most of the interior volume. There was a thick stalk of red tendrils, pulsing like arteries, reaching from the mass to the top of the tank and valve intake.

"What the fuck?"

"Where's the fuel?"

"It's eaten it."

"It's—"

"Yeah, it's eaten it. It's inside the blob in there."

"How do you know?"

"We can't know that."

"So, does this mean we're dead? Out of fuel?"

"We're dead."

"We're not dead until we're dead. We don't know for certain that the fuel isn't in there, just that those things are in there, too. The only way to know for sure is to see if we can regain control of the engine and try to fire it up."

"How could these *things* grow inside the tanks and us not see it on the instruments?"

"We just did."

The screen flipped through different views, all of very similar scenes. There were globular masses within each of the tanks in all four of the refueling rockets carried in the *Ulysses*'s cradle. The tankers were little more than stacks of individual storage units hidden beneath the skin of a rocket. The plumbing to access the resources in those tanks was concentrated in their noses. The cradle ensured a tight fit of the noses to the refueling-capped gantry cranes at the top of the carousel.

And the carousel was surrounded by the forward wheel.

"Paul, get a drone out to the caps."

"Roger, Cal."

Forty-Two

The drone positioned itself directly above the carousel where the refueling caps atop the noses of the tankers nestled into the forward ring. There were red-black vines clearly visible in its searchlights. They wound around the crane arms that held the caps against the tankers' noses and projected in a radial fan to different points on the forward wheel.

The forward wheel, of course, was not actually a simple wheel. It was more of a double-surfaced collar, the outer surface being an open lattice of bracing and supports. There was a veritable web of shining red-blackness lining its interior that gathered into a spray of thickening trunks running up from the inner surface to the collision points.

Forty-Three

"Sonofabitch."

Cal let his eyes flick from face to face in the command module, Sarah to Xu to Inez to the Doc, who shouldn't have been there but was anyway.

"Sonofabitch!"

He realized he was still holding on to his helmet and stuck it to the magnetic rear of Samuels's seat. "Xu."

"Captain?"

"When did this happen?"

"This was not visible from the ship's standard camera views."

Cal hesitated, holding eye contact with Xu for a beat before turning to the image of the engineer on his suit-screen. "So did these connections grow down from the twins or out from the weed in the spindle?"

"I . . . I don't know."

"Paul?"

"I'm not sure Cal, but it seemed like the weed we were originally infected with ran out of steam. If I had to guess, I'd say this new growth comes from the twins and is growing to meet up with the weed, maybe complete some kind of circuit."

"I was thinking something along those lines as well."

"A possibility for sure," said Xu, shrugging his shoulders. "But—"

"We know, it's not the only possibility."

Samuels looked over her shoulder from the command chair and caught Inez's glance.

Cal twisted around and floated toward the rear of the CM, between Xu and Inez's stations. The Doc floated there, still fully suited. Her copper hair was plastered to her forehead. He locked eyes with her and then pulled himself up and out of the CM and into the ship's main corridor. The Doc looked around the space of the module and followed.

Once inside, Cal bounded backwards, requiring her to follow further up the tunnel.

"Xu?" she asked.

"Xu."

"I can see where you'd have some concerns, but I think he's just dreamed of this moment his entire life. It's not going the way he imagined, and I believe he genuinely feels the need to provide a counterpoint to the fear we're all feeling."

Cal stared at the Doc, for longer than he had locked eyes with Xu.

"God knows I'm not going to," she said.

"Thanks, Doc." He propelled himself back into the CM.

Forty-Four

Twelve hours later, there had been no further measurable growth of the red weed anywhere inside or outside of the ship. There had been no unusual instrument readings, no alerts or warnings. Odysseus even returned to annoying them with his schedule of science operations reminders.

Paul Arthor had fallen asleep in his great orange spacesuit, strapped into the foldout seat in front of the engineering ring's valve station. His arms and legs floated, elbows and knees bent, giving the giant man something of the aspect of a baby in the womb.

Cal sailed into the ring, slowing down via handholds and pulling himself to the floor where the engineer was asleep, bobbling against his seatbelt. He touched the big man on his shoulder and said, "Wake up, star-child."

Arthor slowly opened his eyes. "Sorry, Cap'."

"Don't be, we're all exhausted."

"You've had time to talk to control?"

"Yeah."

"What'd they say?"

"They haven't criticized our handling of the situation, so that's good. They're trying to give us advice, but it's pretty obvious that no one knows shit."

"Figured as much."

"We're the ones out here, we keep doing what we're doing."

"How's the world taking it? Aliens and all?"

"Nothing that you couldn't predict. The world's going a little crazy, but it's been dragging on for weeks now, and the public can't pay attention to anything that plays out that long. Not even this."

"So, what now, Cal?"

"I think we're going to go visit one of our new twin friends. So, start thinking about what we'll need, I want you with me."

"Me and not Xu."

"Yeah."

"You think he's losing it?"

"I think he's feeling the strain, and I can't afford that added uncertainty right now. We're going to say that the primary purpose of this EVA is to assess the damage from the collision."

"All right, I buy it."

"But first, go to your bunk and get some sleep. Maybe there's something in the air that the Doc can't find that'll get us, but lack of sleep will kill us both when we're on that thing tomorrow."

"Tomorrow?"

"It's ten o'clock. Tomorrow is in two more hours."

Forty-Five

Cal and Paul Arthor stood with their boots magnetized to the spindle airlock platform. The Doc floated around them like a bee attending to some flowers. Paul locked a set of tools and equipment onto the upper expansion rail of Cal's EVA pack, and Cal did the same for him. These backpacks were bulkier than the ones they'd worn earlier, their housings distended with propellant and thrusters. The Doc handed each of them a round cartridge about a foot wide and a few inches thick.

"The tethers," she said.

The two men nodded.

She handed Cal a small rectangular case. "Sample containers and a collection tool."

Cal gave her a thumbs-up.

"From Xu," she said and handed him a small silver cylinder. She handed a duplicate to Paul. "Cigars, for when you get back."

Cal smiled and said, "You hold them for us."

She unhooked their recharging hoses and reeled them back into the housing. By the time she had turned around, Cal was opening his silver case on the small grated work table next to the suit locker.

"Cal, you aren't."

"I am. Why do you think I forbid Xu from leaving his station?"

Paul looked over Cal's shoulder. "What in the hell is that?"

"Doc, every action taken by this thing, these things, has been one that I can classify as aggressive. You know I'm no hothead, you know I'm open to the possibility that we are facing beings that think very differently from us but—"

"You knew he had that?" Paul asked the Doc, pointing at the gun.

"I value my life, Doc. I value your life, Paul. I value the lives of all humanity. I'm not saying I'm hoping to use this. I'm certainly not, but I have it, and we don't know what we'll find over there. Bringing it along adds to my options."

"What would you have done if the *Ulysses* had been equipped with weapons while at Ceres?"

"This is one of those times you tell me something I don't want to hear by asking me a question. What are you saying, Doc?"

"I'm saying that if you'd had guns on the *Ulysses*, you might have used them to get us out of there, but you didn't and you figured another way out."

"Yes, and a man died. You're not making your point, Doc. I found the damned thing on Ceres."

"Don't take it."

He Velcroed the holster to his right hip.

Forty-Six

Cal stood on the external surface of the forward wheel and watched two drones cross the distance between *Ulysses* and the starboard twin. They had finished a close examination of the impact point, finding the area of penetration completely obscured by the growth of the buttress pylon into the ring structure. The open triangular spans between the wheel's lattice on either side of the impact point had been filled in with a webwork of supporting structures, slowly excreting more filler material. Long, arrow-straight ribbons of tendril ran from the intersection points and down into the carousel.

They took scrapings that turned to ash in the sample containers and turned their attentions to the starboard-side twin; a tapering globularly-cylindrical thing the size of the replacement Statue of Liberty. It was the same color as the blob had been when it had arrived in their airlock, the same color as the tendrils and weeds, the same color as everything except, strangely enough, the original object that had pursued them; its surface having been weathered by eons of radiation exposure and space dust.

The drones finished the crossing, hovering a few feet above the surface of the starboard cylinder. Each unit had towed over a long line and would use their thrusters to provide a stable platform for the two astronauts to cross with the added safety of tethers. Maneuvering units could have done the job alone, but if his years in space had taught him anything it was that you were never sorry to have a lifeline. He snapped his tether to the line and started across. Paul Arthor followed just behind. Cal had a brief flash of childhood memory. A zip line course in Vermont, all trees and green.

The two astronauts crossed the emptiness toward the alien.

Forty-Seven

From the panoramic windows of the docking ring, Xu Zuoren watched the orange and blue spacesuits cross the distance. He was still closed up in his own suit, recharged and ready in case the two needed assistance. He had Paul Arthor's helmet camera feed on a tablet that floated nearby. It afforded a better view, and he glanced at it occasionally. It was possible there would be some form of face to face meeting. If he could not be present, at least he could say that he saw the moment with his own eyes.

The Doctor drifted nearby, watching from the point of view of Cal's helmet cam. Out of the corner of her eye, she occasionally glanced at Xu.

A Quindar tone sounded. "We are aiming toward a point at the prow of the twin. We're going to land on the far side surface and examine the features there, then continue aft in a radial search pattern."

From Paul Arthor's point of view, Cal seemed to be falling toward a grooved, ridged, red-tinged surface of black crystal. He twisted into a crouch, choked up on the tether, and with a spurt of thrusters, pulled himself to the alien surface.

The Doc switched her view back to Cal's camera. Paul Arthor dropped out of the black sky. Beyond his great orange shoulder, the graceful shape of the alien buttress curved insanely away to join with the bulk of the *Ulysses* in the distance.

"We're down," Cal's voice crackled. There was clear electromagnetic interference coming from the twin, confirmed by the telemetry streaming in from both astronauts' suits.

"You going to say anything, Captain?" Paul looked at him through the curve of his helmet. The sun was a cold distant star, and his face would have been in complete shadow but for the lights of the hovering drones. Cal had forgotten himself, Paul remained aware of the moment. He hesitated.

"We come in peace for all humankind."

"Very nice. Classic."

"That says it best, doesn't it? I greet this moment with the optimism of our species." He winked into Paul's camera.

"We are going to take a look at the forward end." Cal rotated and stopped with a few quick thruster bursts and then launched himself slowly over the prow of the garnet twin. From a distance, the forward shape of the alien appeared like a globular rectangle standing on end and flaring out into a spherical collar to taper away into the distance.

Cal skimmed down the face of the twin. It was cross-sectioned by a grid of horizontal and vertical bifurcations. The garnet darkness was, like some of the larger tendrils of the weed, harboring dim, multicolored sparks within.

"Anybody make anything of this?"

The Doc shook her head and looked at Xu, who spoke into his comms. "No clue here, Cal. Just observe as well as you can."

"Roger." Cal piloted his suit around the inner side of the twin, the connecting buttress was about thirty-five feet away. The plan was to return later by descending along the buttress pylon, so Cal made note of features he hadn't noticed earlier before returning to Arthor's position. The engineer was floating parallel to the surface, taking scrapings that turned immediately to ash as they fell into the sample container.

"We are going to start down the long axis of the far side at 4.4 feet per second."

"Roger, Cal. Walking speed."

They swept the far side surface with their searchlights as they leisurely skimmed to the ends of the alien construction.

"It's nearly featureless. It has a glass-like surface similar to the larger roots of the weed."

It took them a little over a minute to travel from the alien's bulbous prow to the tip of its tail. A third of its length ran alongside that of the ship, and yet the maw of *Ulysses*'s engine bell still lay over one hundred feet behind them.

"There have been no breaks in the surface so far, no vents or apertures."

Paul Arthor, this time, flew out over the edge. He inspected the object's tapered rear.

"The tail comes to a vertical wedge interrupted by three stacked conical bulges. No openings to the interior here either." He jetted away, sinking as he angled around to the inboard surface of the titanic cylinder. A quick push from his suit's rear thrusters sent him dropping slowly toward the faraway engine bell, skimming the object's inner flank. Cal appeared over his right shoulder, descending from topside.

"There are what look like vanes here, six horizontal blade-like structures of some kind. No, not blades, more like the dampers on air registers. They run most of the length of the inner surface and are closed up tight."

"Like a closed vent."

The engineer reached out and attempted to move one of the huge vane-like slats, but it would not budge.

"Are they mechanical or organic?" crackled a question over the comms.

"They look mechanical to me, Doc. There are granules in the joints and seams, like a fresh sintering job or 3D print. Excess material that hasn't been knocked loose yet." Arthor dropped closer to the inner surface.

"Are you getting this?"

"It does look mechanical, despite the manner in which it seems to grow. I am convinced this is a machine that is redesigning itself and not an organic being," Xu said.

Cal jetted forward to where the colossal dampers ended. He stared across space to the *Ulysses* and, hundreds of feet beyond, the other alien twin joined to the far side of the ship. The vents on the twin's inner surfaces started just a few feet back from the ship's engine bell.

"Paul, take a look."

"Cal?"

"Do these dampers look like they are placed to interact with the main engine?"

"Like they'll open up and interfere with the exhaust in some way? I was thinking along those lines. These vents are one of the only distinct surface features, so it does beg the question."

"Let's place some cameras here so we can observe the dampers and get back inside." Cal looked down the throat of the *Ulysses*'s plasma engine.

"If it could shut the engine down, it stands to reason it could start it again."

Forty-Eight

"Good news, Xu. You didn't miss anything," Cal said over the comms, removing his helmet and stripping off the EVA backpack within the spindle airlock's vestibule.

He opened the inner door and was presented with a wall of plastic sheeting, fluttering in the null gravity. The sheeting was duct taped, floor to ceiling, and covered every surface. There were two sealed rubber containers with brushes attached to their sides on the sheeting that covered the grated floor.

"What the hell is this?"

"Well," the plastic sheet silhouette of the Doc answered. "It's my first quick pass at some quarantine procedures. The EVA airlock in the docking ring was designed for it. The whole ring is built protein-proof, without cracks or crevices where debris or fluids can hide. Easy to keep clean like the sick bay. This airlock was supposed to be for emergencies only. I'd like to keep any potential contamination contained."

"There's already an alien weed growing in the ship. You think this is really necessary?"

"Are you really arguing with me about quarantine?"

"Not arguing, Doc. Just tired."

"Me too. Just pull the wands out and punch them through the

rubber lids. Swab each other down as best as you can before you come out."

They dusted one another off with the brushes, and a bubbling film fizzed over the surface of their suits. When it had finished foaming, they brushed each other off. Cal looked at the multiple silhouettes and pulled the holster off his hip. He slipped it into the near empty sample container bag and then stepped through the plastic sheeting. The Doc quickly taped it back closed.

"No one got to shake an alien's hand."

"Yet." Paul said with a smirk.

Xu concentrated on helping to remove his backpack, but Cal caught his eyes a couple of times. There was a flash of humility (timidity?) there that he had never glimpsed before. With doubts about himself, Cal didn't relish having to question a crewmember that he relied upon. As he shrugged the backpack off his shoulders, he assessed the man: Xu looked haggard. Like the rest of the crew he was drained, having spent over thirty-six hours now with little or no rest, only liquid foods, and constant stress. Cal decided to attribute his behavior to exhaustion and reevaluate later. If Xu were on the verge of cracking, the others couldn't be far behind.

The Doc was helping Paul Arthor with his backpack. They hadn't taken the extended tool pack off before doffing it, and it was tangling with the harness. The Doctor was still sealed in her suit, with her hair plastered to her forehead and her green eyes appearing sunken and gray.

The crew needed rest. All of them. Regardless of the circumstances, you could push the body only so far. They needed to start a sleep rotation. It was time to adapt to the realities of a situation they had already accepted—they had made contact, and in some way had been captured and boarded by an entity, or *entities*, for unknown purposes.

But they still needed to eat, sleep, and go to the bathroom.

As if to emphasize the fact, the Doc lost her grip on a tool, and it slipped from her glove and bounced off her helmet.

136

Cal raised his left forearm and tabbed his comms. "Mandatory family meeting, Red Hab cafeteria in fifteen minutes."

Forty-Nine

Cal relished the gravitation, leaning hard against the drink dispenser.

"Circumstances may have changed," he announced to his crew with a wry laugh, "but we need to approach this like any other disruption and complete as much of the mission as possible. If, as it seems, we aren't going to die within the next ten minutes, then we need to get back to some basic housekeeping and mission tasks under a kind of modified schedule."

There was a general murmur of agreement.

"All while still working the problem. It's just that, in this case, the problem happens to be aliens."

No one laughed.

"Sorry, folks. We're all tired. But we need to make some plans. First, we have to start to assess the ship, and that means seeing if we can regain control of the firing of the main engine, the RCS, etcetera. Sarah, that's obviously you and Paul."

"Roger, Cal."

"I know you're wiped, but I want you to get started on that right now, aim for a test sometime tomorrow. I want to do this well before we encounter Jupiter's bow shock. And you—" he pointed at Paul Arthor. "I *know* you got some sleep. We have two days until we are due to make the first of our three orbital insertion burns."

"Or else Jupiter slingshots us into oblivion."

"Yes, thanks, Sarah." Cal bowed to his pilot. "You're going to need to get on the horn with control and, assuming the main fires up, see if we can't work up an estimation of the mass of our new additions by comparing the actual versus expected change in our velocity due to the burn."

The two nodded.

"Work up a procedure now, please, then take a look at it with fresh eyes tomorrow morning before we perform the test."

"Yessir."

"Xu, I want you and the Doc to examine the infiltration of those fibers down to the molecular level. I want you to be able to tell me what it's doing across the entire electromagnetic spectrum."

"Yes, Cal."

"But first, I want you both to get some rest."

"I'm okay."

"I said now. To the habs, sleep in your beds. No less than four hours. Go."

The Doc smiled wearily at him through her faceplate.

"No problem."

"Inez, if Xu thinks the actions of the red weed might be more than just an invasion, maybe an attempt to communicate that we don't comprehend, then we need to investigate. I want you to look at the behavior of the weed from that standpoint."

"Yes, sir."

"I'm giving you the option of starting now or taking your four hours. Your choice."

Fifty

Inez let her jumpsuit drop to the floor of her small quarters. She indulged in watching it fall. To Inez, the best feature of the Eureka-class interplanetary ships were the centrifuges. Even around Jupiter, the *Ulysses* EM field generator would provide enough protection from radiation such that the habitats could remain extended and rotating during the months-long exploration of the Jovian system. The encounter with the alien kept *Ulysses* devoid of gravity longer than she'd ever bargained for.

She slipped her nightshirt over her head and again reveled in the feeling of objects under gravity. She hopped into her bunk and asked Odysseus to shut the lights. There was a tiny strip of window material bordering the ceiling, and she watched the stars wheel by as she fell asleep.

Almost fell asleep.

As oblivion encroached, her awareness pushed it back. She sat up.

Fifty-One

Inez entered the docking ring in a fresh jumpsuit. She was alone in the torus-shaped room. She had hoped Xu or the Doc would have been similarly unable to sleep so she could talk with them about their observations of the weed. She floated over to the EVA airlock and the open sections of wall cladding.

She flipped her tablet to the ship's logbooks and the pages for crew notes on the tendrils. As she had suspected, most of the crew had little time or presence of mind to enter their observations, but the Doc and Xu had followed procedure even under trying circumstances, and the video files from the various ship's cameras were all accessible.

She floated over to the airlock window and peered through. There was very little left of the original mass of material that had spilled out of the boarding tunnel. A faint crystalline residue deposited along the tendrils' path of growth was all that remained. She traced the residue to the doorframe to examine the area where it had originally penetrated the seal. The material itself was punctured and distended, yet light from inside the airlock did not seep through. Closer inspection revealed plugs of red-black material stopping up the puncture holes. She tapped one of the plugs with the end of her stylus; it made a loud clack. Solid.

"Odysseus, raise the pressure inside the EVA airlock by 5 percent."

She watched lights blink inside the airlock.

"Pressure raised to twenty-one psi."

She raised her hand over the plugs, feeling for the movement of air. Nothing.

"Is the pressure inside holding?"

"Yes, the pressure inside the EVA airlock is holding at twenty-one psi."

The weed had restored the seal integrity. Despite the mass of the rest of the substance having been . . . redistributed . . . the plugs retained their integrity. That was a possible sign of intelligence, but then again, perhaps the substance was designed to function that way when the pressure changed? If, however, it was a conscious act, would that not also be communication? Observation itself was interaction.

She followed the growth residue behind the wall and into the systems of the ship. She used the tip of her pen to push open the conduits Xu had sliced over a day before. They had been filled with the red weed but were no longer. It was gone. Only trails of ash stuck between the fibers and wires indicated that it had been there at all. She pulled out her ship-phone and turned on its magnifier, leaning in close. It took her a few to find plugs of the red weed material, miniatures of the repairs made to the airlock seal, embedded in some of the pipes. The tendrils had repaired the damage they had caused and had moved on. She opened her own notes window and tapped the voice-to-text button.

"It's like a roving network," she said aloud, yellow text spilling into the logbook window, "reabsorbing and redeploying its mass through new growth elsewhere."

She continued to follow the residue trail, noting again how it had completely avoided the node server. From everything they had seen over the last twenty-four hours the weed growth seemed to be receding forward of the docking ring and expanding down the spindle, as if it had explored the ship for a while before figuring out where it wanted to go.

Inez opened the hatch to the spindle and drifted down into the

142

red-tinged industrial corridor. The weed here curled in between conduit, pipe, and wire; sections of it had formed into turgid bulbs, luminescent sparks circulating beneath their surfaces.

She opened the notes page, scrolled to the video of the EVA to the cradle node, and saw the same behavior. The weed neatly avoided the node—the interface between the ship's computer network and its peripherals.

"Cal, are you awake?"

"I am now."

"I have a weird idea."

Fifty-Two

Inez climbed the ladder down from Red Hab's cafeteria and into the closet-sized hallway next to the captain's quarters. She reached out and knocked on the door.

A muffled "Come in" filtered through the thin material.

She accordioned the door open and stepped into the near dark of Cal's quarters. A slip of windows overhead spilled starlight, sending shadows to crawl across every surface. Cal was curled under his covers, only the mop of his hair protruding over the soft foam of his pillow.

"I have an idea," she said.

"It'd better be good."

"I think so."

Cal rolled over under his covers, his eyes peeking up over the blanket.

"Lay it on me."

"So, I've been frustrated since the start of this. It seemed like I didn't have anything to do. Anything I tried led to no response and the weed avoids anything that's my responsibility. Except maybe a bunch of wires."

"And?"

"And I started to fall asleep and for the first time thought to ask why that was."

"Xu thought maybe it was avoiding anything that might be a thinking being; us and the computers."

"Maybe, but maybe the behavior itself is communication? Maybe it's trying to suggest a response?"

Cal sat up in his bunk. "What kind of response?"

"It's avoiding the one system that would almost certainly engender communication, while exploring or infiltrating everything else."

"So, it's either not interested or it isn't capable of talking to us."

"Or maybe it's asking us to take the final step."

"What do you mean?"

"What if we set up another server, an isolated server, and connect it to the weed? Physically connect it. Make the one connection it won't make itself."

"To what end?"

"Communications! We have Odysseus port into that server and attempt to be our intermediary."

"How are we supposed to connect, jam wires into it?"

"Pretty much, yes. It knows how to grow into our wires and cables."

Cal was unconsciously shaking his head in agreement. "And it already knows how to interact with our systems well enough to abort the firing of the main."

"Exactly."

Fifty-Three

Inez pulled a backup server out of a storage locker and Velcroed it onto the workbench, plugging it in quickly to ensure that it powered up correctly. As it booted, she floated over to the equipment locker to unplug a battery power unit from its charging station. A full charge would power the server for weeks, and the unit sported an external connection to recharge while running. Should the experiment last that long.

The node server started up fine, she shut it down and strapped it to the battery unit.

Xu, Cal, and the Doc were waiting for her in the docking ring.

"What do you think you're going to do?" The Doc looked genuinely concerned, as if the few hours of sleep signified a return to normalcy, and Inez's suggestion would tip things back toward chaos.

Inez held up a stripped length of cable leading to one of the server inputs.

"And then what? You're going to hook Odysseus up to it? You don't think that's risky?"

"I've loaded the server's drive with information control suggested we try exchanging in the event we make contact. Odysseus can port in wirelessly and help it try and understand. Full black-level safeguards."

"If it wanted to infiltrate Odysseus, it would have already," Cal said.

Xu held the server in position while Inez aligned its connector to one of the regular attachment points along the spine. A few connectors below, she anchored the power supply and plugged in the server. An auxiliary display built into the side of the case lit up as the new node came to life.

"Are you going to load some form of interface in which to attempt to communicate?" Xu asked.

"No, I think the thing to do is to let it explore the node server and its files and see what happens."

"I agree," said Cal. "It's adapted to everything else, why not this?"

"Maybe because it's tried everything to avoid doing what you're about to make it do?"

"Or it's an opportunity, Doc. It's worth a try."

Inez took the stripped end of the cable in her hand and held it over one of the jet-red bulbs of scintillating lights. She hesitated.

Cal nodded.

Inez laid the bare cable against the surface of the distended root. The crystal-hard surface seemed to accept it, flow around it. Inez tugged gently, but the wire held fast to the glassy surface.

Inez turned to Cal with a smile that lit up the corridor.

"Was our invitation accepted?"

"Maybe." Xu rubbed the folds of his jumpsuit sleeve and looked closely at the juncture of wire and weed. "It's sinking deeper into the tendril." He held his ship-phone up to magnify the alien interface. "Delicate roots are already growing."

Cal looked to Inez. She shrugged her shoulders.

The server restarted.

She turned to Cal. "Invitation accepted."

Over the general comms channel and through every speaker in the ship, the pilot's voice rang out. "Prepare for maneuvers, I hope."

Fifty-Four

"Paul?"

Pilot Sarah Samuels was in the command seat preparing to test their control over the ship.

"Paul? Checks complete."

"I'm here," the big man replied from the engineer ring. "Let's go. Reaction control system first and then I'll clear out, and you can try and burp the main."

"All right, I'm going to rotate the ship by five degrees and halt rotation." She reached out to her console. Three identical circles encompassing silhouettes of the *Ulysses* dominated the screen. She reached out and rotated the y-axis dial.

All along the length of the ship, the RCS thrusters flared, setting the ship into a slow spin around her long axis.

"Rolling to starboard. Y plus-five degrees."

"It's working." Cal entered the CM, floating forward and sliding into the empty righthand seat. Apart from the visual cue of Jupiter rolling around outside the cockpit windows, the movement of the ship was imperceptible.

"Looks like we have control."

"The RCS is a completely different system from the main, though."

"First things first." Her attention never left the silhouette of the ship on her control screen. It shifted toward plus-five on the y-axis and slowed and stopped as thrusters fired to halt the rotation.

"So far, so good."

"You want me to run her through the works or just burp the main?"

Cal looked at her. "Burp the main."

She locked eyes with him. "Paul, clear out. We're going to fire."

"I'm outta here," Arthor replied over the comms.

"Here we go. She pulled the controls console to her and wrapped her fingers around the hand controller. With her left hand, she passed over the three luminous dials she'd paid so much attention to earlier and placed a finger on a glowing red chevron. She pushed the slider up to 80 percent thrust and held her finger down on the command button in order to set the burn timer.

"Thirty seconds."

"Transmitting log to control."

She opened the startup checklist on a new display window.

"Propellant injectors?"

"Check." This time, Cal provided confirmation rather than the synthesized voice of Odysseus.

"RF generator one?"

"Check."

"Helicon coupler?"

"Check."

"Superconducting magnet array?"

"Check."

"Ion cyclotron heater coupling?"

"Cheeeeeeck."

She shot him a glance, which he repulsed with a smile. She smiled back.

"RF generator two?"

"Check."

"Magnetic confinement nozzle?"

"Check."

"Reactor output?"

"361 megawatts at 72 percent efficiency."

"Up a point . . . Twenty-two seconds to main engine ignition."

Samuels moved another control tab to maximum.

"EM field to full."

"Ten."

"Injectors on." She swiped a button on the display.

The valves opened; hydrogen gas flooded into the cylindrical titanium chamber.

"Nine seconds."

"RF generator one operating. Helicon at 99 percent."

A heavy antenna wrapped around the engine cylinder began to hum. Radio waves whipped the hydrogen gas, converting it to plasma by ripping electrons away. The temperature inside the engine soared to exceed that of the surface of the sun.

"Seven."

"Throttling RF. High thrust, low specific impulse." Sarah twisted a glowing dial on her touchscreen.

The superconducting magnets around the cylinder squeezed the newly generated plasma, accelerating it through the engine.

"Second RF up."

"Five."

"Ion cyclotron powered."

The engine's second antenna coil bathed the engine in radio waves, confining its electromagnetic field and setting up a resonance within the plasma. The temperature in the engine soared to almost two million degrees Fahrenheit.

"Three seconds."

"Magnetic confinement nozzle collimated."

"One."

The countdown timer expired, and she squeezed the trigger.

"Ignition."

The ions and electrons corkscrewed through the engine, into the expanding magnetic nozzle and out to space. A luminous cone expanded into being inside the *Ulysses*'s engine bell . . .

And roared into a massive torrent of blue-white flame.

Fifty-Five

Inez felt the main engine kick while she was gazing through the airlock window, keeping a watch on the server mounted to the spindle corridor wall. She gently bumped against the hatch. Just inside, the server restarted itself for the third time.

Lights in the chassis blinked on and off.

After a moment, the fan stopped and started again.

A few seconds later, she could sense that the engine had shut down, the slight rearward current that had pushed her up against the hatchway window had ceased.

The node server restarted again.

This time, the screen did not load to the operating system prompt.

This time, the screen remained dark.

The status lights inside the case strobed and blinked. First, at random. On and off. Then all at once. On and off. Then in a chase of eight lights followed by another chase of eight lights, in simple animation.

Then the server restarted. Again.

Fifty-Six

"What's it doing?" Cal asked, staring at the bulging trunk of blood-black tendril into which the wire from the node server vanished. It was awash with multicolored splinters. Xu and Inez floated in contemplation of the experiment.

"My guess is that it is exploring the architecture. Learning how the devices that make up the server are controlled," replied Inez.

"Is this a good thing?" Samuels swam in through the hatch.

"It proves that it can connect with and use elements of our technology," said Xu.

"Perhaps a mixed blessing," said the Doc.

"So, you're saying that we were able to fire the engine only because it let us?"

"Yes. That's what I'm saying," Xu answered.

Cal turned to Inez. "So, are we in communication with something?"

"I don't know. There's some kind of understanding going on, for sure. It was able to shut down the main engine. I'm willing to bet that wasn't an accident. I think it already understands the electrical basis upon which our computers function."

"On, off. Binary. I would suppose from its viewpoint, the basic organization of the binary data—bits, bytes, packets, would be the hardest part," said Xu.

"I think it's moved beyond that." Inez tilted the monitor screen and swiped alongside to raise the volume. Variations in hiss and static came over the speakers. "I'm recording all of this, by the way."

She pushed away from the node to consider it from the opposite side of the spindle. "It's advanced to the point where it can activate the monitor and produce noise through the speakers."

"Is it trying to talk to us?"

"It's just turning them on and off, sending random signals through them. I see no sign of any understanding of the *purpose* of these devices. No sign, for example, that it grasps that the monitor can be used to display content to others."

"It may not understand the concept of *other*, despite the behavior we are observing."

Samuels held up her fingers and made the quotations sign. "Observing."

"Or it could be attempting to communicate in ways that we just aren't noticing. Maybe something within the static?"

"I'm looking," answered Inez.

"If it can control one of our computer systems, then it is safe to assume that it understands our mathematical calculative nomenclature. Binary numerals, additional subtraction, equal to, not equal, greater than, less than," Xu said.

"Mathematical calculative nomenclature."

"Yes."

"And if it understands those things?"

"Hopefully, it will talk to us."

"Hopefully."

Fifty-Seven

The Doc settled into the command module's empty right-hand seat and smiled at the pilot.

"So, good news, finally!" she said excitedly.

The pilot shrugged.

"C'mon, Sarah. You've got control of the ship, and we have made some sort of contact with the *thing*. Things are starting to break our way."

"Nothing's broken our way yet, Doc."

"You're too negative."

"Doc, how do we make a burn when we don't know what its effect will be?"

"What do you mean? Because of the things in the tanks?"

"Yes and no. What I mean is that we calculate our engine burns based, among other things, on the mass of the *Ulysses*. With that thing attached to us, we don't know what our mass really is. We might not have enough fuel or time, or both, to brake that mass into Jupiter orbit.

"Well, what the hell are we going to do?"

"This is why Cal wanted us to test the engine as soon as possible. We're going to have to wait for some data from control. The Deep Space Network will be able to accurately measure our change in velocity. We know how much we *should* have accelerated based on the original mass of the *Ulysses* minus burned consumables. By comparing how much our velocity should have changed versus how much it *did* we should be able to get a fairly accurate mass estimate for the alien."

"And you're waiting for that now?"

"Yeah, that and for Paul to get back to me on these gauges. I'm not getting proper tank volume readings up here."

"It's been over an hour since the test."

"Yeah. Control should have received our messages by now. We'll hear back in another hour or so."

"And then you recalculate the engine firing and find out whether we're already dead or not?"

"Yup."

Fifty-Eight

Paul Arthor was in the engineering ring, sitting in front of the window that separated him from the fuel system's valve controls and gauges. He had the video feed from the cameras inside the tankers up on his console again. The alien bladders had grown ever more turgid, filling most of the cameras' fields of view and blotting out his vision of the spherical tanks' reflective interiors.

He tapped the drone control window to bring it to the front. The exterior drone was where he had left it, sailing alongside *Ulysses*'s carousel and giving him a good view of the caps of the rocket tankers where they connected to the refueling armatures. The fibrous branches of weed that had grown over the armatures had swollen together and fused into larger trunks, penetrating the caps and their reinforced hoses.

He lifted his head and glowered at the gauges.

"Sarah?" he called into the comms.

"Paul, whaddya got for me?"

"Did you receive the delta-vee figures from control?"

"Yes, Odysseus is checking the new calculations right now, but as you know, we have a variable that we can't solve for."

"I know, Sarah."

Well? What's our propellant situation? What's going on with these readings?"

"You're not going to like it, same answer as before."

"Which was?"

"There's nothing wrong with your equipment. I'm reading the tank pressure right off the internal gauges."

"Paul, they read *full*."

"I know."

"They weren't full before, they're certainly not full now. After another burn."

"I know, I've checked the engineering cams. The ones that are still working show those bladders as having expanded. The tanks read full, but we know they aren't."

"And we have no idea what those bladder things are doing?"

"None. I'm afraid. We will have to take tank values somewhat as a given."

"Say again?"

"At this moment, I have no way to understand what's going on in the tanks, and every minute brings us closer to Jupiter."

Samuels grimaced.

"On the positive side, the engine did fire. So, even though the cameras say *empty with monster guts* while the gauges say *full*, I figure it's gotta be something in between."

"We're going to *guess*?"

"We are going to take into account the new mass value extrapolated from our delta-vee change and then *assume* that the volume in the tanks is what it would have been without whatever's going on inside the tankers."

"Why would we do that? Just go on like everything is normal when it isn't?"

"Talk to Cal, but I don't know what else there is *to* do. We can ostensibly control the ship and make the burn . . . and we have to make the burn. So, I'd rather wait to start poking around at that thing until *after* we're in Jupiter orbit."

She frowned at him.

"And we can monitor the tanks during maneuvers and see if we can get meaningful readings out of them. See how much propellent the sensors say we used and again compare that to the theoretical."

"I guess that makes sense."

"I'm pretty tired. I hope I'm not missing something."

"So do I."

"And that's my plan. Recalibrate the instruments so that they reflect where the tank volumes would be if things were normal."

"And see what happens."

"Yeah."

"And what if it did eat our fuel and we're empty?"

"Then they'll talk about us forever. Ghost ship *Ulysses.*"

Fifty-Nine

"Hey," Inez called to Xu over the general comms channel. "Mister calculative nomenclature, I think it's learned your math lesson." She floated in the mouth of the spindle with Cal.

Crenellated towers and fractal swirls washed across the quarantined "embassy" server's screen, phasing through different color sets.

The Doc poked her head through the hatch. "It's making that? On the screen?"

"Yeah."

"What does it mean?"

"We don't know," Cal replied.

"Is it the same pattern?"

"Pattern of what?"

"Of the shapes on the original object. The moonlet, the probe."

"Probably, or at least governed by some similar fractal equation."

"Communication?"

Cal turned to his science officer. "Xu?"

"It's communication," Xu said.

On the screen, the fractal cyclone began to stutter, as if the system was bogging down under intense activity. As the staccato swirl chugged around the monitor, various pixels remained illuminated. Within thirty seconds, the swirl had shrunk to nothing and a set of images had resolved, side by side. A set of images of the *Ulysses*.

"Holy shit."

"Communication," Xu whispered.

"I thought you said that was impossible without a common frame of reference?" the Doc asked.

"That's what it's doing now! Don't you see?" The Comms officer pointed. "On the left, that's the stock photo of the Eureka -class ships from the files on the server. Next to it is an image of the *Ulysses,* but it's from the object's viewpoint. Taken, it looks, sometime during its original approach."

Xu nervously ran his hand up and down his opposite sleeve. "Our attempts at communication . . . We were starting with mathematics and equations . . . Its approach is to try and define a common perception of reality. I believe it is asking, *does this image and my image represent the same thing?*"

"You said it understands our . . . mathematical calculative nomenclature?"

"Yes. I suggest we use mathematical notation to respond *equal to,*" Xu continued.

"Agreed," Cal said.

"Mathematical calculative nomenclature, Jeebus." Samuels flashed a smile at Xu, whose face relaxed into a grin.

"How do we do that? What's binary for equal to?"

"Can we just use the keys?"

"If it understands the computer architecture, would it understand the keyboard input?"

"Try it."

Inez opened a panel on the server and unrolled the auxiliary field input strip. She brought up the command line and entered an equal sign.

"If we are correct, I anticipate the next set of images will expound on the last," Xu said.

Nothing happened.

"Again?"

"Give it time."

"How long do we wait?"

Almost as soon as the Doc finished speaking, the stock image of the Eureka-class collapsed into a whorl of pixels, which spent itself constructing another image, clearly sourced from the camera on the node server. It showed a contemporaneous view of the crew, crammed into the spindle to watch the exchange. On the right, the image of the *Ulysses* remained.

"Another equation?"

"What's the answer to this one?" Samuels asked.

"Greater than," said the Doc.

Cal looked at her. "Yes. Greater than."

Inez tabbed in the greater than symbol.

Xu marveled. "Think of how unexpectedly effective this communication has been in just two interrogative rounds. Do you see what it is doing? It's the answer to Lem's Dilemma. The lack of common reference points. It's creating its own. We have established what we are and which of the entities it has encountered is the primary of the two. The machine or the biological. All without the translation of a single word of language."

Sixty

Cal and the Doc sank gently through the extended centrifuge arm. They landed on the hab's ceiling and climbed through the hatch and down into the heavier gravity of the ship's sick bay level.

The Doc slid open the thin door to her office, and the two of them stepped inside. She dropped slowly into the chair behind her desk and pulled the Velcro seatbelt across. From a bottom drawer, she produced a squeeze-bulb topped bottle.

"Cliché, I know."

"I like clichés. Give me a belt."

The Doc's office had one of the best windows on the ship, but she kept its shade drawn whenever the habitat was rotating, which suited Cal just fine. She squeezed a few fingers of bourbon up into the bulb, pulled it off the top and batted it over toward Cal. He squeezed it into his mouth and tossed the bulb back.

The Doc replaced it onto the bottle and drew herself up a shot.

"You ever think, Doc, about how so much of spaceflight, so much of just *living*, is just trying to buy yourself a little more time?"

"A little more time for what?"

"A little more time for luck, opportunity, for some new piece of information to help you project yourself a little bit further into the future."

She tossed him the bulb again.

"You need another one."

Cal laughed.

"So, what now?"

"Everyone gets some more rest. Then we prepare for the first orbital insertion burn while you, Xu, and Inez keep trying to talk to our new friend."

Sixty-One

Ulysses had been traveling within Jupiter's sphere of influence for weeks, but now the Earth vessel was approaching the steeper slopes of the massive world's gravity well. More than two million miles from the outermost limits of the planet's swirling atmosphere, the ship was finally entering Jupiter space.

Space is vast and lonely, but it is by no means empty. The sun's magnetic field floods the solar system with an interplanetary medium; a thin ion soup blown out by the dynamic pressure of the solar wind.

Jupiter orbits within a hollow in the solar wind carved out by its own magnetic field. A field so powerful that it shoulders its way millions of miles inward against the power of its own parent star. The solar wind flows around the massive cavity and blows Jupiter's remaining magnetosphere into a tail that stretches beyond the orbit of Saturn.

The Doc remembered the background info. It was not her realm of expertise, but anyone chosen to crew a Eureka-class ship had to know enough of the other disciplines to be able to step in and adequately fill another's role.

"So, what's it going to be like?"

They were all in their suits again, but she held her helmet in her hand and drifted into the aisle next to Samuels in the CM's command seat.

"Jupiter's bow shock is like a sonic boom," Cal said, floating up behind her. "The solar wind blows out at about a million miles an hour, and where it hits an obstacle, there's turbulence."

"And in this case, the obstacle is the biggest one there is. Jupiter's magnetosphere."

Cal, helmet also off, zero-G sidled past her and slid into the right-hand command seat. "We can listen to the sound it makes." He turned on the cockpit speakers. A strange radio signal squeaked and warbled.

"Kinda eerie."

"Distance to Jupiter's magnetopause?"

"We should be entering it now," said the pilot. "Exact boundary distance unknown."

The magnetosphere was a massive teardrop shape, and they were approaching it at its shallowest point.

"Fluxgate magnetometers operating normally. Proximate star cameras aligned."

Cal glanced back at the Doc. "The magnetometer is like a compass in that it tells the direction of a magnetic field, but it also gives you the magnitude, but you need precise location data for it to work." He turned to the pilot. "Launch a feeler probe."

He turned back to the Doc and continued, "Star cameras determine the exact positioning of the ship in space by checking against known star positions."

Samuels slid a tray out from her console and flipped open a shielded button.

"Launching feeler probe."

There was a vibration as a small radiation-hardened device was kinetically launched from *Ulysses*'s nose. The single-use instrument would streak ahead and give them advance knowledge of the complex boundary they were about to transition and the environment within.

"Feeler reporting sixteen particles of solar wind plasma per cubic inch. Seventeen."

"This should be a gentle transition, but there are currents within the bow shock, so we're going to do our best to ride the path of least resistance, electromagnetically."

"Feeler reporting through the bow shock. Down to four particles per cubic inch and dropping."

"We're in the magnetosheath."

"The solar wind is mostly blocked by the magnetosphere at this point. It's going to vanish entirely once we're inside, but the rad levels are going to jump again once we start entering Jupiter's own radiation zones."

The Doc stared at the Jovian planet through the great curving window, still so far away.

The weird squeaking screech over the speakers was suddenly swamped by the sound of a staticky tornado.

"We're through."

"Through what?"

"The bow shock."

"That's it?"

"That's it."

Cal punched a number of lights that appeared on his console. Images of the planet's various electromagnetic topographies rotated on the screen.

"We are within the protection of Jupiter's internal magnetic field now. The solar wind can't touch us but—"

"But Jupiter is about to roast us," Samuels said.

The *Ulysses* sped inwards toward Jupiter.

"Prepare to reorient for Jovian orbital insertion burn."

A shower of bright sparks burst in front of the ship, causing them all to involuntarily jump. Samuels laughed.

"Micrometeoroid deflected by *Ulysses*'s EM field," said Cal. "Good time to haul in the habitats and ramp up the EM field's spin."

Cal's gloved fingers danced over the screen, and he broadcast into the general comms channel, "Prepare to retract the centrifuge arms."

The golden skin of the centrifuge arms crinkled and folded. The habitats were pulled in, the total width of the arms shrinking from five hundred feet to less than one hundred. The protective EM field contracted and tightened around the ship.

"RCS pressures are reading normal. Main engine pressures are . . . whatever they are."

Cal looked at the pilot sideways.

"X plus 180 degrees, point the engine into our direction of travel."

The thrusters flared and the *Ulysses* pitched over and around, slowing to stop, hurtling backwards toward Jupiter.

"Odysseus, main engine initialization procedure start. Power to propellant injectors."

The Doc pulled out the jump seat and strapped herself in.

Cal opened the general comms again. "Helmets on, people." He closed the channel, muted the cockpit chatter, and opened his private line to Inez.

"How are things going in preschool?"

"Just continuing on with the lessons."

"Any reaction to us starting the engine?"

"None that I can tell. No sign of agitation or anything."

"Has it displayed any other new images?"

"No, Cal, it's just running through the image files control suggested. So far, the only thing it responds to are these mathematical operations. Greater than, less than, equal to, additive, subtractive. I don't know what kind of map of relationships its drawing from this—or what kind of communication could possibly result."

"Keep at it, but from the other side of the docking ring hatch. We're about to fire the main. Call me if anything weird goes on. I'll send Xu back to you as soon as possible."

"Roger, Cal."

Cal turned his external mics back on at the instant Samuels said the word *ignition*.

The thrust from the main engine forcefully pushed him back into the padding of his seat. The sky outside the window was a bowl of stars, the planet being almost directly behind them.

"Throttling back from high thrust to high impulse."

The pressure against the seats eased; the *Ulysses*'s burn would continue for hours, slowing the ship and allowing it to fall ever more into the grip of the Jovian planet's gravity.

"How long before we make orbit?"

"We're kinda already in orbit, Doc," said the pilot.

"What do you mean?"

"What she means is that the burn that's occurring is warping the orbit we are on into a highly elliptical one that passes over the poles to avoid the worst of the radiation."

"We are inside the protection of the planet's magnetic field, though?"

"Yeah, but where Earth's field helps make it a paradise, Jupiter's deflects the solar wind but traps something far worse—intense radiation pouring from the Jupiter-Io flux."

"Which is what, again?"

"Most of the magnetic field is generated by electrical currents formed by Jupiter's rotating core and the rotation of the storm bands in the outer atmosphere. However, volcanic eruptions on Io eject lots of sulfur dioxide into space. This gas forms a large torus around the planet."

"Where the worst of the radiation is produced. That I do remember."

"Right, the magnetic field forces the torus to rotate in the same direction and at the same angular velocity as the planet, throwing plasma into the magnetic field and producing radiation a million times more intense than Earth's Van Allen belts."

"And when should we be hitting these intensified zones?"

"We'll pass through a few, but the orbit is calculated to miss or just skip through the big ones. *Ulysses*'s shields can handle limited exposure

170

to even the most intense zones. We should already be detecting the increased radiation."

"But we aren't."

"Come again?"

Cal checked the dosimeter readings on his console. They had steadily risen from nearly zero in the magnetopause to the equivalent of 0.1 millisieverts per day, about the same exposure as an outer Galilean moon.

"I've got nothing." The Doc showed him her suit-screen. Her dosimeters read flat. "Zip."

Cal smiled, looking at her screen. "That's because you're reading interior dose, Doc." He pointed at his console. "I'm taking my reading from the dosimeter on the feeler probe. It's outside the *Ulysses's* protective EM field."

She cocked her head and frowned at him. "Cal," she said and tapped her suit-screen. Her green-gloved index finger pointed at her medical configuration. There were two readings for radiation dose. One was the interior sensor, but the second was from the dosimeter on the antenna mast. The mast rose out from the ship and beyond the EM field. On it was mounted a variety of hardened instruments and the communications gear. The dosimeter on the mast should have been reading the outside environment. It should have read the same as that of the feeler. It didn't.

"Motherfucker," said Cal.

"Well, at least this isn't a bad thing."

"How so? I need to be able to trust my craft, Doc."

"Well, assuming the readings are real, it's a good effect . . . or result. Is all I meant."

"Paul?"

"Yeah, Cal?"

"What's up with these EM field readings?"

"Checking, but I'm reading the time lapse, and the only pattern I see in the EM field matches absorption of the main drive output."

"Meaning?"

"Meaning nothing else is hitting the field. So, either the entire outer radiation environment of Jupiter has vanished—"

"Or our hitchhiker has its own EM field generator."

"It would make sense."

Cal cast his eyes up at the Doc. "Thanks, Paul."

"Like I said, at least it's a positive," she said.

Cal trained his eyes forward, which of course was backwards to the direction he was heading. That was spaceflight in a nutshell, he thought.

Sixty-Two

Unseen on the surface of each of the alien booms that attached themselves to *Ulysses,* pustules began to form: egg-like clusters growing, rising up through the skin of each vast boom.

Sixty-Three

"Open the main screen, rear view. Let's see where we're going," said Cal.

The screen between the two windows folded open, doubling its size and descending to obscure the view of empty space presented by the panoramic windows.

There was the gas giant. Shockingly large and growing larger, filling the screen. A blue-white corona of flame danced around the rim of the engine bell, sending eerie shadows toward them, which danced across the inner faces of the alien booms—the only part of the alien constructions visible to the camera. The main continued to fire. The ship was slowing down and falling deeper into Jupiter's grip.

"We're going to come in fast and very low over the atmosphere on our first orbit. About five thousand miles above the clouds and below the worst of the radiation torus. Then we'll sweep around Jupiter and back out on a high ellipse. At that point we will start making burns timed to circularize our orbit while keeping out of the worst of the soup."

Ass-backwards into the unknown, Cal mused. "As we pass through the planet's radiation zones, Odysseus will constantly be repositioning the ship, angling it to keep the bulk of the liquid hydrogen in the tankers between us and the radiation source."

Sarah pursed her lips. "A long and fuel-intensive maneuver and a total leap of faith right now considering we don't even know if there's anything in those tanks to shield us—which is the whole reason for constantly angling the ship in the first place."

"Not the time, Sarah. After we're in orbit. Right now, as long as the engines fire, we'll continue to act as if everything is normal. As bizarre and disquieting as that may seem."

The ship was streaking in toward the gas giant, its south polar surface slowly rolling into view. The tenuous ring system caught the dim light of the sun and revealed itself as a wispy and perfect circle. Aurorae coursed out over the planet's surface, haloing the pole. Brilliant blue arcs snaked up and folded back into the clouds.

The main engine shut down on schedule. The first of the three planned burns was complete.

Ulysses would shoot over the pole, headed for the equatorial belts where huge swarms of electrons are accelerated nearly to the speed of light by the magnetic forces of the planet. "Here come the fireworks," said Cal.

The Doctor leaned back. The rear-view image on the screen was so clear that it was like looking out a window. More and more electrons began to strike, ricocheting off their EM shield.

"Feeler probes indicate we are passing through wave after wave of increasingly energetic particles."

Washes of sparkling motes broke against the field, and then waves of greater and greater intensity struck until the entire view was drowned in a constant plasmatic haze. A heartbeat later the haze receded. Sheets of luminous embers shrank to a spattering of sparks only to begin ramping up again a few moments later.

"This will only get more and more intense as we near the equator."

"That doesn't look real," whispered the pilot, pointing at the curve of Jupiter.

The counter rotating belts and zones of atmosphere vanished at the southern pole, subsumed into a realm of hurricanes. An unnaturally geometric arrangement of swirling atmospheric vortexes: a literal pentagon of cyclones the size of worlds rotating around the planet's axis.

"But it is," said Xu. "A natural and enduring atmospheric structure formed by atmospheric disruption. The polar cyclones are a critical component of the planet's electric dynamo, the heart of its magnetic field."

They watched the atmosphere organize itself with the precision of ancient clockwork.

"The turbulence powers the motion of the cyclonic polar gears and, in turn, the gears generate the magnetic field that powers the turbulence," Xu said at a near whisper. He was awestruck.

The south polar region grew larger in the view. The vortexes radiated an intense blue-white light, swirling darker and darker in toward the eyes of the storms. Bright buffer zones of counter rotating gas encircled the storms, stabilizing them. An ouroboros of swirling atmosphere. With no surface features to disturb or drag against the currents of gas, the general arrangement of storms would endure as long as terrestrial formations of rock.

The exact southern pole of the planet was encircled by the maw of a massive central hurricane larger than the diameter of Mars. The monster storm was surrounded by the slowly shifting and rotating pentagon of cyclones.

"The bigger ones are between twenty-five hundred and four thousand miles wide. If you notice, there is a smaller cyclone forming on the periphery. On subsequent orbits, we might witness the birth of a sixth south polar storm," Xu said.

"That would be the big news of the mission, if it weren't for you-know-what."

"In about an hour, at the speeds we are going, we'll pass over the north pole and you'll see aurora and an atmospheric show that should be even more impressive than this one. Eight cyclones circling an even larger central hurricane."

Winds up to three hundred miles per hour whipped cold clouds of methane, hydrogen sulfide, water, and trace compounds up thousands of miles, mixing them into endlessly swirling storms. The southernmost red gas band vanished, swept under white clouds of ammonia snow that lent the king of worlds an unfamiliar appearance.

The speed of the rotating bands was startling to see, Jupiter's day was the shortest in the solar system. The giant world rotated around its axis in under ten Earth hours. The rapid spin causes the planet to bulge at the equator and flatten at the poles. The clouds seemed to ride just feet beneath the speeding craft's planet-facing viewports. Constant winds kicked up incredible swirls and painterly dabs of atmosphere. It was almost impossible to take in the mesmerizing patterns of churning gasses, folding into patterns of such strange complexity that the eye recoiled. The Doc was reminded of the deepest fractal gyrations of the alien. She had to blink her eyes and refocus on the whole of the Jovian, away from the dizzying details.

The cockpit speakers crackled with ghostly sounding transmissions. Radio wave emissions emanating from somewhere above the planet.

"Jupiter is singing to us."

"I wish it wouldn't."

Most of the atmosphere existed in great circular bands rotating counterclockwise around the planet while others, spectacularly, ran in reverse. White spots marked the crests of enormous waves surging along the cloud surface. Colored striations, plumes of sulfur and phosphorus gas, rose from the superheated core. The relatively tiny space vehicle and its mysterious hitchhiker soared thousands of miles above swirling storms propelled by heat from far below that unleashed lighting far larger and stronger than any seen on Earth.

Cal's personal comm channel beeped. He looked at his suit-screen; it was Inez. He switched over. The Doc and the pilot both looked over at him.

"Cal, please look at this." An image of the pole appeared. "This just came up on the alien's monitor."

"It's tapped into our cameras again?"

"That's the north pole, there are eight surrounding storms," said the Doc.

"She's right," said Inez into Cal's ear. "And we haven't been there yet."

"So, where'd it get the photo?"

"From the server. An old NASA photo."

"Why's it showing it to us now?"

"Exactly what I want to know. Why?"

Sixty-Four

"The engine is powering up."

"What?"

"Injectors, RF generators, helicon. Everything. Powering up."

"Paul!"

"I don't know what's going on, Cal!"

"Whatever it is, stop it. If that engine ignites, it's going to drop our orbit lower and lower. At the altitude we're flying, we don't have much room for error, if we lose too much velocity, we are going to hit the atmosphere."

"You don't have to tell me, Cal!"

Paul Arthor, in his great orange suit, yanked open the hatch into the spindle. A hatch that, while the main engine was powered, would only be opened under the direst of circumstances. He leapt into the spindle, pulling the hatch closed behind him.

The main engine fired.

"Paul!"

No answer.

"Sarah, thrusters. Turn the ship around, maybe the alien will cut the main."

"Roger, Cal." She tapped the X-axis control and twisted, but the

RCS refused to respond. She stared at Cal but didn't say a word.

The engine continued to fire.

Xu twisted off his helmet, letting it float away.

"Xu, what are you doing!" Cal shouted.

The science officer looked dazed. "Cal, if this burn continues more than four minutes . . . It's a deorbit burn."

Sixty-Five

The *Ulysses* streaked backwards over the gas giant, riding a pillar of plasma flame. As the craft's velocity decreased, it fell faster and further into the grip of Jupiter's gravity, dragging it down closer and closer into a tighter orbit over the planet's atmosphere. Slowing down and speeding up.

The command module was silent save for equipment sounds and vibrations. Cal's eyes periodically swept the interior and held each crew member's gaze briefly. The engine had been burning for more than five minutes.

Powerful winds flowing in opposite directions blew across the surface, reaching speeds of more than 220 miles per hour. The alternating bright and dark bands had their origins deep inside the planet. The movement of such tremendous amounts of matter altered the gravity of the planet, leading to an imbalance between northern and southern hemispheres. The gravity varied from pole to pole. *Ulysses* shuddered and jounced violently.

They watched as a rotating vortex corkscrewed into a whirlpool, opening a chasm into deeper layers of the atmosphere.

"Look at that," the Doc whispered with morbid curiosity.

"Odd gravitational events occur over roughly one-twentieth of the planet's surface, including turbulent jet streams that stretch down through multiple atmospheric layers," Xu replied.

They were getting closer to the equator. The ship's augmented electromagnetic shield fizzed and popped as torrents of particles washed over it in increasing frequency. In the rear view, the lights dimmed on the prows of the twin alien cylinders. *Why would it be devoting such energy keeping us alive, only to kill us by crushing us in a fall into Jupiter's atmosphere?* Cal puzzled. He watched the orbital plot update.

They were dead.

Sixty-Six

Ulysses flew over the equator and in through the most intense belts of radiation in the solar system. The window in front of Cal swept up and across the starboard side of the cockpit and so, to his right, he could see the dizzying bands of Jupiter's cloud tops now just three thousand miles from his right shoulder. Across the module, beyond the window and over the pilot's shoulder, floated an otherworldly sphere. Jupiter's innermost moon, Io, a mottled yellow world stained with red. Had things gone differently, they would have eventually swung by Io and dropped autonomous probes to its surface.

But that would never happen now.

Volcanoes on the moon blasted more than two thousand pounds of sulfur dioxide into Jupiter orbit every second. Atoms of the gas, constantly ionized by electron impact and ultraviolet radiation, fed plasma into the magnetosphere.

The ship's electromagnetic field blazed, flared, and then started to fade as they came through the worst of the equatorial radiation zones.

Sixty-Seven

Paul Arthor floated on floor two of the engineering ring, halfway down the length of the reactor housing. Before him was the armored hatchway into the depths of the nuclear power plant. Beyond that hatch, the heavy cover over the fuel rods. Winding up and around the housing and running all over the module, the myriad coils and lengths of piping that utilized the heat output of the power plant to warm the ship. It also cooled the reactor and powered the electrolysis unit that fed life support with oxygen.

The power plant was running at 100 percent, producing 366 megawatts of power, the engine consuming much of it by stripping electrons from hydrogen, pouring plasma into the superconducting accelerator.

He raised his forearm screen and opened the comms channel.

"Cal, I can't stop it."

The Doc reacted before Cal. "Paul! Are you all right? What's your dose?"

"We can worry about that later, Doc."

"It's too late, Paul."

Paul refused to acknowledge Cal's statement and continued, "Not without physically pulling the control rods from the reactor. The system doesn't respond to local computer commands, I tried closing the valves to the hydrogen tanks manually, and the computer re-opens them immediately. There's a blip in total power output, but there's too much of a buffer built in for it to matter."

"It's okay, Paul."

Cal thought about what he said. *That's interesting, though . . . The alien was in control of the ship, but it needed the ship for some reason. It wasn't using its own propulsion system, the one that had allowed it to pursue and catch them. It was using* Ulysses*'s engine and power plant. Perhaps that suggested limits to the alien's power? That the alien was powerful enough to control but not overwhelm them? Or maybe its energies were occupied elsewhere?*

Sixty-Eight

Ulysses streaked down over the northern latitudes. They were only a little more than one thousand miles from the tops of the thunderheads, and the world was suffused with blue light. Streamers cast distinct shadows on cloud structures far below. The northernmost storm bands leaked upward toward the pole, swirling together to supply the storms with the mechanical energy to churn into electrical currents connecting the polar region with the magnetosphere.

Along the dorsal surface of the alien devices connected to the Earth ship, pustules had been breaking. Swelling, popping, ejecting a multitude of spherical globules in their wake. As with any such endeavor, some would continue to orbit for a time, some would burn up in the atmosphere, but most would retain the proper velocity to make it into the ring system.

Ulysses's drive flame sparkled as the ship continued to shed horizontal velocity, dropping beneath the ribbons of charged particles that swept across the polar horizon. High-energy electrons raced along the planet's magnetic field and into the upper atmosphere. They excited the gases there to glow across the entire electromagnetic spectrum: Jupiter's northern aurora. Sweeping curtains of light silhouetting the Earth ship's descent.

186

Sixty-Nine

The clockwork system of storms swallowed the horizon, stretching thousands upon thousands of miles and extending beyond the boundaries of the rear-view screen. The screen glow and the light from the cockpit windows lit the command module in opposing patterns of blue light. A hundred Earths would be swallowed, insignificant against the churning vortexes. Cal stared out through his helmet, mouth agape. His eyes flickered to the red-orange glow of the map created by infrared cameras and magnetometers. There, the colossal cyclones and anticyclones looked like a tangle of fiery octopi.

Every camera and instrument on the ship was active, Xu was making sure that the *Ulysses* sent as much telemetry back to control as possible even though the EM field was likely blocking their transmissions.

They were dropping faster now, falling below five hundred miles from the atmospheric surface. The engine was firing directly toward the central hurricane. The storms flowed below them, looking more like chasm walls than miles-long streamers of gas.

Cal watched as the horizontal velocity indicator dropped to zero. The ship was just over one hundred miles above the clouds. The engine cut off immediately. As the ship plummeted toward the atmosphere, the RCS thundered into life, *Ulysses* pitched 180 degrees, it's nose and grand front windows falling to face directly into the maw of the central storm.

The engine restarted, erupting into full thrust. A shining cone of fire pointing straight along the Jovian's north pole and out toward the stars sprang from *Ulysses*'s tail. The ship accelerated straight down the planet's axis. Straight through the nexus of the dynamo and the planet's electromagnetic field. Straight into the eye of the central polar storm.

With the engine firing, Cal knew that they would cross the remaining distance to hit the outer atmosphere in seconds. The *Ulysses* wouldn't last long after that. Either atmospheric friction would melt the vessel or the weight of the atmosphere would crush them. In truth, both.

This was it. *This is how I end*, he thought. Cal had never felt so small. Time seemed to slow down so he could take it all in. What was happening seemed to interweave itself between all that was. Like all the days of his life intersecting. Surprised, he felt grateful. For the experience of it all. Life. And this. This. What a way to go. Good job, Calvin Jensen Scott.

He smiled sadly. This was it. *It.*

But he didn't want to go.

The ship couldn't survive a plunge into the atmosphere. There was simply no way out.

Or maybe there was.

Maybe?

He could still hope.

The flush of heat vanished from his back. The pit in his stomach fled. Hope was a helluva thing. The electromagnetic field in front of them effervesced. He stared into the maw.

Seventy

There was an incredibly loud crack as the spacecraft hit the atmosphere. The field arced and sparkled. Cal clenched his teeth and girded his bowels. There was no point in not retaining his dignity. A moan ran the length of the ship and was followed by a shudder that Cal felt sure was the ship beginning to tear itself apart. But the ship did not tear itself apart.

It should be tearing itself apart.

But it wasn't.

There was a thunderous rumbling around the vessel, and another sound. Not quite the shrieks of atmosphere but close. He felt the nose of the ship pitch up and a sick feeling blossom in his stomach that he had not felt in years. The pull of real gravity, gnawing at him in his seat.

The ship was descending, impossibly, beneath the surface of Jupiter's outer atmosphere. The environment of the *Ulysses* was utterly transformed. Space had vanished, and the vessel sank through what was clearly *sky*. Twisted ribbons of darker and heavier gas, miles-long, created topologies within the azure "air."

All around them, the scale of events was just beyond the capacity to fully comprehend. Turbining walls of gas spooled around them hundreds of miles in the distance. Far, far below, further away than the diameter of entire worlds, perspective vanished into the vast cyclonic maw. They were falling through the electrical dynamo of Jupiter's magnetic field.

As Cal blinked himself back into conscious control of his thoughts, awareness of his body returned to him. They had somehow survived the interface with the troposphere and were descending into the planet's atmosphere.

The field sparked and crackled. *Ulysses* was angling away from the center of the eye, drifting toward the cyclonic winds. They dropped toward a bank of vermilion thunderheads, no doubt many times the width of the Earth. Lightning flashed between towering structures of gas.

"We're not dead." Cal opened the comms to his engineer. "Paul, were not dead. Get the hell out of there."

"Roger, Cal."

The ship's nose hit the outer boundaries of the heavier gas. The shield sparkled into a violent glow, revealing its shape as a flattened conical wedge completely enveloping the ship's prow. Looking down the flanks of the ship through the docking window, Cal could see the sparkling limits of the alien shield stretching back as far as he could see. The vanes along the internal surfaces of the cylindrical alien devices had opened. Crimson light was spilling out. The *Ulysses* moaned as it bucked and rattled.

"Jesus! Fly this boat, Samuels!"

"I'm sorry! I wasn't even thinking." The truth was that she was shocked to be alive.

Ulysses heeled to port as the windward edge of Blue Hab began to drag against the outermost wisps of the denser crimson gas.

The engine throttled into *afterburner* mode.

"The alien's trying to steer with the throttle!"

"It's lost control of the RCS!"

"Or just needs your help," said Cal.

Lightning ahead fizzed between canyons of cloudbanks.

"This ship was never meant for an atmosphere."

"Well, it's in one now. The alien is clearly protecting us or we'd already be dead, but we obviously can't rely on it for everything."

Another jolt.

"It doesn't understand how fragile we are!"

"RCS primed!" Sarah jammed the hand controller to the side, firing thrusters all down the ship's flank. *Ulysses* edged laterally out from the red streamer. "She's flying like a cannonball!"

"Let's see if we're really working together or not!" The pilot reached out and rotated the X-axis control dial. *Ulysses* swept around, bringing its nose up and tail down. The engine suddenly lit again, blue-white plasma roaring out from the engine bell. The ship's rate of descent began to fall.

"Dear Lord, we are working together, aren't we?"

"This has *got* to be eating up a lot of fuel."

"Yes."

"Showing on the indicators?"

"No."

"Jeebus."

"Maybe it really is providing us with unlimited fuel?"

"We'd better not count on that."

"Well, I don't know what we can possibly do about it. We don't have—"

The ship's nose broke through an unavoidable streamer of twisting orange gas. A huge jolt wracked the ship.

"—wings."

"Extend the habitats!"

"Cal, the arms will be torn apart by the winds."

"Sarah, we should already have been torn apart. Let's see how far we can stretch this protective field."

"Wings?"

"Wings. Extending the habitats, 10 percent," Cal said, swiping his hands along the controls. The angular living spaces extended into the field twenty feet to either side of the ship. Visible because of the sparks from the impact of particulates in the atmosphere, Cal watched the field stretch to accommodate the habitat's expanded volume. It was as if the ship was inside an otherwise invisible balloon, pushing out against the skin. He threw the habitat control window over to her console. It flowered open in front of the pilot, and she rotated the habitats to maximize lift.

"How's she feel?"

"Better?"

"More?"

"Can we?"

Cal thought about that, at some point that invisible balloon could break. "We didn't know we could do what we just did until we did it."

"More, then."

Cal extended the arms by another 10 percent. *Ulysses* vibrated. Sarah banked the habitats.

"Better."

Unseen and far below them, swirling gases produced both acoustic and gravitational waves. Wave collisions released tremendous plumes of heat. Huge thermals and hotspots rose from the nested storms, a twisting hydra of heat geometry that buffeted the ship.

Ulysses creaked like a sailing vessel. The resultant addition of lift caused the ship to buck and soar as it hit a rising bank of hotter air. The ship had become the spine of a kite composed of shining electromagnetic pinpricks and a tail of blue plasma flame.

The alien throttled down the engine.

"Odysseus, overlay the magnetometer and infrared onto the cloudscapes, please." Her HUD shifted, allowing her to see the heat rising from below and the direction of the magnetic flux. She banked the habs and the alien powered up the drive to 60 percent. The shaking decreased measurably.

"We've caught a monster jet stream."

"Well, let's stay inside it."

"I think that's what our friend had in mind."

"Is it possible we might survive this?" the Doc asked.

"Doc, you got me. We shouldn't be alive."

"Can you imagine the power of the electromagnetic field that it must be generating?"

The ship shuddered and dropped, banking through a great arcing curve. *Ulysses* was inside the atmosphere, but it was still on an elliptical orbit, corkscrewing ever inwards around the planet's core.

"I would imagine this jet stream is created by gravitational as well as atmospheric forces," Xu said, holding onto the frame of his console and staring at his screens.

"That's crazy," said the Doc.

"Not at all, there can be eddies and currents in gravity, just like in liquid and gases. It would make sense for them to align. *Ulysses* creates a gravitational force via rotation. The movement of all those counter rotating storm bands that now surround us does the same on a much larger scale."

A terrible creaking moan snaked up from somewhere deep inside the vessel.

Sound like a thousand hailstones hitting a tin roof hammered across the shield, illuminating it with a million staccato starbursts.

The Doc blinked. "That looked like . . . rain?"

"Hydrogen and helium don't always mix well. Helium rainstorms occur all across the interior of the planet. They literally alter the magnetic field."

"Or it could have been frozen ammonia," Cal said without taking his eyes from the cockpit windows.

Ulysses banked with the flow of the jet stream, corkscrewing around the eye of the hurricane. There was a coruscating blue flash; they were dropping toward a funnel within a funnel, carried by the jet stream, down its throat.

"What was that!"

194

"Similar to the storm we saw growing around the south pole."

"But what was that flash?"

"I don't know. Lightning? Related to the aurorae perhaps?"

The ship bucked and shook.

"It may be that the jet stream we are traveling through is a permanent atmospheric feature, like the polar storms, the aurora. A stable arrangement of chaotic ingredients."

"You don't think this is a natural phenomenon?" Cal asked.

"I don't. I think these storms were, at some point, deliberately seeded or diverted in order to create this effect and that we will see further evidence of atmospheric engineering as we go deeper."

Cal looked him in the eye, pursing his lips.

"And you think our alien friend is part of this system?"

"Yes, why else are we still alive?"

"You think we're going in, huh?"

"Oh yeah."

"Yeah, me too."

"All the way down, I'm guessing."

Seventy-One

Ulysses moaned, and its electromagnetic field erupted in a luminous wave as the pressure around the ship increased. There were no plans or procedures for him to call upon, but Cal had the full complement of instrument readings open in front of him. He tossed their windows up against a cutaway of Jupiter from the server's files.

The server.

So preoccupied with not being dead, he had almost forgotten about the thing that was most likely responsible.

"Inez?"

"I'm still here, Cal."

"Us too, incredibly. It seems our friend has plans."

"None that it's confided to me."

"Is it still talking?"

"No, Cal. It seems busy."

"Hang tight down there."

"I will. Are we going to die or not?"

"I don't know, but not if I can help it."

Cal closed the tab. His attention returned to the Jupiter cutaway; he had to guess at where they might be. The feeler probe had long since been crushed. There was, thankfully, no part of the ship that extended beyond its alien-augmented field, but that also meant that the picture that filtered in to *Ulysses*'s instruments was distorted. He had no idea how the values for wind speed or external pressures that he was seeing related to reality.

The view from the panoramic capsule windows was an ever-changing current of blue-violet hues and whip-whirling streamers. Winds buffeted the ship. They had been in powered descent for minutes now . . . He had to admit that there was no way he could tell where they were going or how fast they were getting there. No way to tell what was going to happen next.

"Burning up fuel at a good clip, Cal."

He glanced at his pilot and shrugged his shoulders.

The blue hues were deepening. Light was bleeding out of the sky.

The prow of the ship broke through a massive cloudbank. A kaleidoscopic ripple of sound and light danced over the shields. Cal peered up and around, following a multitude of sparks as physical objects struck and skittered across the electromagnetic barrier.

"Those looked like crystals."

"Diamonds. We must be very deep in the atmosphere where showers of compressed carbon can form between the denser layers."

The ship shook and listed to starboard as it seemed to reverse in its arcing course.

"How are we not being crushed?" the Doc asked again, marveling.

There was a ghostly whine as the engine throttled up even further.

"Cal," the pilot whispered.

He looked over at her, and she nodded at the fuel gauge. It had finally started dropping. So, there were limits after all.

The cerulean shades of the whipping atmosphere grew dark, mottled by turbinations of slate gray and streaks of obsidian. Another vibration hit. A shower of diamond ricochets washed over the ship, punctuated by a burst of lightning that momentarily restored detail to the cloudscapes.

The ship banked again, to port this time. There was a sensation of lateral motion as if the ship were sliding over the air currents. Ahead of them clouds thickened, flowing like streamers of heavy cream over and around the nose. There was a darkness approaching. A density.

Vortices rose out of the dark. Samuels banked the habitats as the RCS thrusters barked. Liquid hydrogen rain swirled up into the gaseous hydrogen and helium layers and twisted into a hurricane to port. *Ulysses* pushed off to starboard following the jet stream current.

The engine throttled back and stopped.

"Are we out of fuel?"

"Propellant."

"No, reading just above 50 percent in the tanks."

The ship struck a boundary, and its structure rang like a gong. Cal's head bounced against the inside of his helmet in a way that reminded him of Bart Henry.

Both rear consoles restarted. One of Xu's screens didn't come back on, so he gripped it in his red gloved hand and gave it a shake. In front of them their EM field sizzled. Squinting through the luminous haze colored the scene in yellowed hues. The ship was encapsulated within a current of darkly translucent and reflective fluid that had merged into the jet stream. It was not as though they had entered a new space so much as they were following a groove along the same shape, now made from a new and different substance.

The engine started again, ramping quickly up to full thrust.

"Keep us in the center of the current, Sarah."

"Roger, Cal."

The RCS thrusters flared in rhythmic bursts.

"The pressures down here, they're immense," Xu stammered. "We are getting closer to the core. The hydrogen is compressed into liquid. We're inside a sea of hydrogen."

Cal leaned forward, straining against the bonds of his harness, to follow fleeting geometries formed as the current interacted with the surrounding liquid flow. They were within a river within a sea.

He could not tell how quickly they were moving, there was nothing by which to judge. None of *Ulysses*'s instruments extended beyond the field, and any probe they launched would be crushed in a nanosecond. The turbulent interactions he was gawking at could be just beyond the transparent window or hundreds of miles away.

By any stretch of the imagination, they had to be moving at an incredible speed, the main had been firing nearly the entire time. And they had to be orbiting or else they'd have passed right through the planet by now. He was convinced that *Ulysses* was in an elliptical slingshot orbit, looping through the planet, getting closer and closer to the core.

Ahead, areas of brightness exploded and faded away.

"What was that?"

"It's possible it was a form lightning."

"Liquid thunderstorms?"

"Not exactly, but theoretically, as you get toward the core the pressure becomes so great that it squeezes electrons off the hydrogen atoms and allows the sea to conduct electricity."

"Like liquid metal."

"Yes."

There was another reflective flash, much brighter this time. It coruscated down the jet stream, momentarily revealing the flowing current as if it were a solid structure. There were variations within the simmering gas that conducted the arcs of electricity in different ways; streamers of bonded plasma scaffolding the maelstrom.

Ulysses rocked and shuddered with the turbulence. None of the external sensing instruments worked, but Sarah Samuels was a pilot. She learned to fly quadcopters off the rooftops of Boston when she was a girl. She flew classic turboprops in her teens. They all could feel the increased gravitation that was penetrating the EM field, but she could feel its movement. Her gut was a magnetometer. She knew where the field was going, and she drove the *Ulysses* through it.

A sheet of electricity washed through the rushing fluidic environment, sparking around the ship. *Ulysses* banked to starboard, and the darkness in front of the hurtling vessel seemed to resolve into a death-black sphere. This was the seething heart of the hydrogen sea. The core of the planet.

Xu's scientific curiosity would not be contained; he unstrapped and flung himself across from the gawking Doctor and between the two command seats, gripping the headrest of each with his gloved hands.

"Is that?"

They were wheeling around the featureless inky globe. They seemed to be moving at incredible speed.

"Is that the core?"

"What is it!"

"Liquid or solid?"

A secondary set of luminescent ripples erupted a few feet inside the shield and vanished.

"Energetic particles getting through the alien shield!"

"Confirmed, I'm reading increased absorption levels by our native field."

"How much do you think our field can help?"

A huge vibration struck through the ship. Screens along the right side of the command module blinked off. Cal's entire console went dark.

Coming up over the horizon, covering the surface of the sphere was a system of fractal shapes. Eight massive cyclones rotating around a central hurricane mapped in two dimensions on the shining dark surface of Jupiter's core.

The *Ulysses* accelerated.

Seventy-Two

The biological mind simply becomes overwhelmed. Devolved into reaction alone and then beyond the capability of conscious thought. Odysseus was able to function longer, attempting to fly the ship, which turned out to be impossible.

Seventy-Three

There was a strange smell in his nostrils, the taste of bile in his throat. It felt like the crust of sleep was upon his eyes, it was an effort to open them. Cal blinked rapidly to break his eyelids free, unable to rub them through his faceplate.

Out through the windows was bright sky darkening to black above. Huge banks of storm clouds stretched as far as the eye could see, throwing lightning down into the lower layers of the gas giant's atmosphere. Brilliant curtains of shining auroral sheaths stretched wide across the crest of the world. Stars twinkled beyond.

Cal looked behind them, out the docking windows. The field sparkled, the starboard alien object, at least, was still attached. He looked up at the still illuminated rear-view screen. The vanes on the inner surfaces of the twins were closing. The scintillating lights on their forward ends had somehow resolved into a ring of lights forming an opening to the interior of each cylindrical device. Gases streamed into the orifices.

Ulysses was thundering upwards, on a ballistic trajectory through the thinning atmosphere.

"Sarah!" Cal cried out. He reached over and shoved her. Xu was crumpled in the rear of the module. The Doc lolled against her jump seat restraints. "Sarah!"

The pilot blinked under her helmet. She looked at him wide-eyed and then out at the panorama rushing toward them.

"Fly, Sarah! Fly!"

She grabbed the hand controller, RCS system coming alive. The central screen lit back up next. She stabbed out at multiple glowing buttons. The system faithfully restarted. She slid the control tab forward, and the engine throttled up into high thrust mode. *Ulysses* danced on its plasma exhaust, propelling itself up and out of the gas giant's troposphere. The sparkling interactions with the protective EM field faded away to an intermittent flash.

The *Ulysses* erupted from the atmosphere of the Jovian planet trailing a cascade of churning gas. The openings on the forward ends of the alien cylinders had closed, reforming into a matrix of lights. The engine blasted plasma out behind them. She began to draw down the control tab, throttling back the engine as it became apparent that they had miraculously achieved orbit: they were falling around the atmosphere of the gas giant so fast that they continually missed its surface.

She dropped back into the cushions of her seat. Wheezing to take a breath. The hydrogen tanks read full again.

Cal looked at her, stunned. The Doc began to stir.

There was something wrong with Jupiter. It had changed its appearance. The giant world had somehow shed its counter-rotating bands of orange, red, and white gas and taken on a paler yellow hue. The planet's storms swirled into densities of green gas instead of red. Haloing the entire horizon was a highly reflective ring system reminiscent of Saturn's but striated differently. The rings were split into three distinct and fairly equal hoops likely consisting of countless tiny particles of water or ammonia ice. The outer ring seemed to have an inclusion within it that created a turbulent band.

Far off, the sun, a sun, shone with surprising brightness revealing a large moon hidden in shadow. They were so close that Cal could see a shimmering border leaking blue-green light around the newly glimpsed sphere. It almost certainly had an atmosphere.

Sliding from the moon's shadow was another. A vast orbiting disc-like shape that cast an oval shadow of its own down across the illuminated shoulder of the moon.

TO BE CONTINUED IN BOOK THREE: THE ODYSSEY
Available now!
The Odyssey: Wine Dark Deep: Book Three
Learn more:
https://www.amazon.com/dp/B08BWYPPX5/ref=cm_sw_em_r_mt_dp_D
d5kFbH1D9J57

Made in the USA
Monee, IL
12 April 2021